For Marie and Lance Lanese with aloha,

Russ Cahill

KOLEA
A STORY OF HAWAI'I AND BEYOND

RUSSELL CAHILL

Booktrope Editions
Seattle WA 2015

Cover Design by Gwen Gades
Edited by Elizabeth Flynn

This is a work of fiction. Names, characters, places, brands, media, and incidents are either the product of the author's imagination or are used fictitiously. Any resemblance to similarly named places or to persons living or deceased is unintentional.

Print ISBN 978-1-5137-0121-9
EPUB ISBN 978-1-5137-0142-4
Library of Congress Control Number: 2015910349

CAST OF CHARACTERS

Aalaonaona: Known as Aala, a landless royal who has borne a king's child outside of marriage. Her name means *fragrant one*

Haunani: Uulani's daughter. Her name means *beautiful tree*

Ho'okelo: Navigator and canoe instructor

Iaea: Chief of Halawa on Molokai

Ka'atoowa'a: Known as Ka'a, a Tlingit woman

Kahuna kalai wa'a: Priest canoe builder

Kalani: A large young man

Kanaka wai wai: A chief of Oahu

Keiki Loa'a: A Haida boy found by the Hawai'ians. His name means *Found Child*

Kepa: A young man, a tuna fisherman of Oahu

Kili: Son of Pualani and Kalani

Koa Ko'i: Great warrior and lua fighter blinded in battle, he is Pueo's husband and a weapons maker. His name means A*xe Soldier*

Kolea: Child of Aala and the king of Maui, his name means *Golden Plover*

La'a kea: Daughter of Ka'a and Pa'akiki

Mahi: Son of Nanoa, and Kolea's half brother

Makanunui: Son of Iaea. His name means *Big Eyes*

Nanoa: King of Maui

Naukana: Chief of Oahu

Nene'au kai: Son of Kolea and Haunani

Pa'akiki: Tough, unyielding. A small man with a deep voice

Pa'ao: Ancient priest

Pualani: A large and powerful woman. Her name means *Flower of Heaven*

Pueo Luahine: A hula practitioner descended from the original Hawai'ian warrior priests. She is a shape changer, has an ability to see the future, and is adept at close combat. Also known as the Old Owl Woman

T'ooch': Ka'a's brother, a Tlingit warrior

Uulani: Principal weaver and sail maker in Halawa. Her name means *Star of Heaven*

Waahia: Pueo's teacher and mentor

Wot: Chumash chief

INTRODUCTION

Long before the magical fingers of Jake Shimabukuro danced across the strings of an ukulele, and before the pure notes of Israel Kamakawiwo'ole enchanted listeners, and before the Matson ships docked at the Aloha Tower carrying the vanguard of what would become an army of tourists, and long before American merchants locked the last ruler of a free Hawai'i, Queen Liliuokalani, in Hulihee Palace and, with the support of United States Marines, took over her government, and before the coming of religions bent on saving the souls of the rapidly dwindling population, and before common colds, measles, and influenza laid waste to a huge percentage of the native population—these Hawai'ian islands, farther from a major land mass than any on Earth, were discovered by a fisherman.

On a voyage two or three thousand miles from his home in the Marquesan Islands, a man named Hawai'i Loa came upon these islands that had sprung from a crack in the sea bottom. He returned home, gathered his family and some crewmembers, and traveled back to settle this new land. The Big Island of Hawai'i is named for him. The other islands are named either for his children or his crew.

At a time when many European sailors were wary of getting too far from land for fear that they would sail off the edge of the planet, many voyages were being made by intrepid Polynesian explorers in great double-hulled canoes between Hawai'i and the Marquesas, Tahiti, Easter Island and New Zealand.

This story is about the people who traveled north to Hawai'i. Could they have gone even farther north? That is my speculation. *Kolea* is the story of the people of my tenth great-grandmother. The places in this story are real. The people have been prisoners in my imagination for the past 45 years and I have finally decided to allow them to escape.

ACKNOWLEDGMENTS

In 1973, on a tour of Hawai'i with the Honokohau-Kaloko committee, I was encouraged by Kumu Hula, Iolani Luahini (Harriet Makekau 1915 – 1978), to write this book. She loved the idea of the Pueo character. Sam Ka'ai of Maui taught me about lua fighting, canoe building and about being Hawai'ian. Susie Cahill (1938-1982) walked and climbed throughout the mountains of East Maui with me and talked about the genesis of this story. Lynn Wallen, retired Museum Curator, helped me envision the Alaska Native people in the story. My sister Robin Connors, an archaeologist who spent two tours of duty at Kalaupapa, Molokai, helped me with Hawai'ian culture.

The following people read and criticized early drafts: Kim Benish, Skip Wallen, Marty Pinnix, Matthew, Adrianna, Tim and Susan Cahill, Joan Gallagher, Hana Cahill, and my writing and social media guru, Suzanne Shaw. Molly Gallagher typed my first hand written manuscript. To my wife Narda Pierce, who shared a magical night in the Haleakala Crater with me, thanks for the encouragement. To my Booktrope team of Elizabeth Flynn, Gwen Gades, Ross Hardy and Sarah Strawinski a big thank you.

The characters portrayed in Kolea are figments of my imagination. This is a work of fiction and any resemblance to persons living or dead is coincidental.

—Russell Cahill, 2015

CHAPTER 1

THE ECHO OF LAUGHTER rang off the cliffs as the naked girls swam through the stream like fish, pulling one another under the surface and splashing. The carefree children sunned themselves until they were dry and then fastened their pa-u about their waists and strode up the trail toward the village of Kaupo.

The eyes that watched from the heavy vegetation alongside the cliff noticed many things. The girls wore the yellow feather decorations of the ali'i and were evidently daughters of chiefs. Their laughter indicated a lifting of the kapu that had kept the people in their houses for the past eight days.

After a glance around, the slender figure emerged from the bushes and headed for the pool. Except for her long graying hair, the figure could have been mistaken for that of an athletic boy. But the surefooted movements of the old woman were tempered by a grace that could be identified with only one profession in the kingdom of Maui: she was a dancer.

The clothing she wore was in contrast to the graceful movements of her body. On her feet were thick sandals woven from the leaves of the hala tree. The pa-u that hung from her hips was fashioned from a coarse kapa, beaten from the bark of the wauke bush, and dyed with the colors of the forest in which she lived.

The little woman set down the net bag she carried in her arms, unslung the calabash that had been over her shoulder, and carefully removed her clothing. She washed the garments and stretched them on a rock to dry and then dove into the sun-warmed pool and swam about, washing herself in the clear waters. When she had finished, she emerged from the water, picked up her things, walked up the hidden trail to a sunny spot, and lay down to dry.

After she had dried herself, the woman gathered some fresh breadfruit and walked to the flat stone where she had left the ihe spear—but it was no longer there. It had been a great one, long and heavy, meant for defense, not throwing. The ihe was gone, as she expected, and in its place were several packages of food and various small items of barter. The woman gathered the items into her bag and began the long hike back up the mountain.

She ascended through small irrigated patches of taro and then through fields of sweet potatoes. Climbing higher still, she entered the tree line where the ohia-lehua grew, and farther on into the great koa forest of Mana wai nui. As she passed the locals, they averted their eyes. Part of that was from respect, but the other part was fear. It was believed that many of the great Hawai'ian dancers of her time were enchantresses.

The lengthy hike she was making would have tired even a great warrior, but it bothered her not at all. Her legs were conditioned to the arduous hula. She could chant and dance for hours at the shouted cadences of the ancient language of her gods. Each morning and night from the cliffside home she shared with her man, her chants and dances went out to Laka, the god of dance. When weather conditions were right, the sound carried down to the village and brought tears of joy to the old people and fearful apprehension to those young people who did not know her. "The owl speaks," the old people would say.

And indeed she would: Pueo Luahine, the Owl Woman, would speak and her voice would float down the valley, making its way into the ears of the people below.

* * *

The blind have an acute sense of hearing, so Ko'i could hear her as she came down the secret trail to the ledge on which they made their home. She smiled as she came into the little clearing. Although he could not see her do so, he smiled in return. "What have you brought, Pueo?" he asked.

"Ahh, "she said, and her voice conveyed her happiness. "Your spearmaking has been rewarded well. I have some salt, and taro, as well as two knives and some sharks' teeth." He held out his hand, and she placed the knives onto his palm.

His face brightened as he hefted the stone knives. He judged that they would be excellent for shaving down the hafts of the spears he fashioned from the hardwoods around their home.

Ko'i had not always been a weapons maker. Once he had been called Koa Ko'i, the Axe Soldier. As the tales of his expertise spread, the locals had simply begun to call him Axe. In his youth, he had been a lua fighter, trained in the arts of hand-to-hand combat. He was a champion among champions: one of those who guarded the king and who fought preliminary individual battles before the armies closed in for general warfare. Ko'i was not as tall as most lua fighters, but he was broad. His scarred arms hung from his shoulders like the limbs of a kukui tree and his thighs and calves resembled the trunk.

Back then, Ko'i's specialty had been the stone war axes. He could swing one in each hand. His technique was simple: he would swing one at the head of his opponent and another at the legs. For a dozen years he was undefeated. And then, in a great battle on Kauiki in Hana, he had stayed behind to cover the king's retreat. Swinging his two axes, he had felled five soldiers from the island of Hawai'i, but then two others had gotten a noose around one of his legs and yanked him off his feet.

As he fought to stand again, the invading war chief had gouged out Ko'i's eyes and had flung him from the cliff onto the rocks below, leaving him for dead.

Pueo had been in Hana, had heard of the incident and had hurried to the foot of the cliff, where she found Ko'i nearly dead. She had waited until it was dark, stolen a canoe, and brought him back to Kaupo.

After Ko'i had healed, the king of Maui had offered him a job training lua fighters, but his pride would not allow it. So when he could travel again, Pueo had led him to their hideaway on the ledge and since then, he had spent his days fashioning tools and weapons for other warriors.

His years as a fighter did not go away easily. On some nights Pueo would hear him thrashing about in his sleep, and she knew that in his dreams, he still defended his king.

CHAPTER 2

THE AROMA FROM the imu ground oven made Ko'i's mouth water. Pueo had been cooking for several hours, and the food smelled ready. As if she had read his thoughts, Pueo pulled off the leaves and pieces of bark that covered the food cooking on the hot stones in the imu. Carefully, she lifted the food from the ti leaves. She carried food to the blind man and then carried hers to her own place.

The two ate separately. For a warrior to eat with women was forbidden by the kapu. Pueo respected the kapu, and Ko'i respected the idiosyncrasies of his woman's chosen profession. They had not spoken of it, but he knew she would be going on a journey. She had gathered a lot of food and accompanied him into the forest to forage for a large supply of firewood so he could remain at their home on the ledge in her absence.

Ko'i had heard her chanting the ancient chant a few days before. He had not understood it, but then, few could have. The words were known only to the priests and dancers of the tradition she followed. She didn't make these chants often, and when she did, they were always followed by long periods of silence as if she were listening to an answering voice. Sometimes the chants followed a visit from one of the owls that hunted in the grassland above the ledge. Two nights before, Ko'i had heard the high-pitched scream of the hunting owl, and Pueo had begun her chant shortly afterward.

"I am going," Pueo told him. "I will bring you a gift when I return." Ko'i nodded and embraced her. She kissed him on his neck beneath his ear, and she climbed the trail to the cliff top. At the juncture where the cliff top intersected their trail, she turned uphill and began to climb even higher. As she walked into the rainforest, she spread a cape about her shoulders for protection.

On the first part of the journey, Pueo followed the wild pig trails near the cliff side. The koa trees grew wide branches that closed into a great forest canopy. In some places, the tree cover was so dense the sky was not visible at all. As she climbed, the trees grew shorter but denser. Strange and wonderful flowers thrived in this forest, and marvelous birds, driven to this isolated place by feather hunters, were everywhere. The i'iwi were most common. The brilliant vermillion birds would land on the flower vines and stick their long curved beaks into the flowers to extract their nectar. An occasional o'o would show its yellow tufts as it flew its black body through the forests, but Pueo knew they were becoming rare.

Three hours later the old woman walked out of the forest into the alpine grasslands. The sun was going down, and she found a cave in which to spend the night. Gathering large bundles of the dry grass, she made herself a nest in the cave. Later, she walked to the lava outcropping above her cave and began a slow chant to prepare herself as the sun dropped behind the ridge above her.

In the darkness of predawn, after an uncomfortable night, Pueo continued her journey up the ridge. At dawn she stood on the great flat stone Pohaku Palaha. From this stone, the lands of East Maui were divided and parceled out to the chiefs. The kingdom was secure with one exception. Soldiers from the army of the island of Hawai'i held the fortress of Kauiki in Hana. From there they foraged into the neighboring districts, killing, looting, and pillaging the countryside.

But Pueo's mind was not on the occupation. The scene from the ridge on which she stood was striking. To the south she could see the island of Hawai'i with its twin snow-covered peaks. To the east and north were the green slopes of windward Maui. Perhaps most striking of all was the view a few steps to the west, the great crater of Haleakala.

The people of these islands held the crater in awe. They told stories of how Maui, the demigod, had snared the sun from within the crater. Pueo knew the stories well, but she also knew that behind the stories there existed a powerful body of spiritual strength, strength that manifested itself to her now. Her body trembled as the clouds, driven by the wind, arose in front of her—and stopped.

The sunlight streaming out of the sea silhouetted her body on the cloud and a small rainbow surrounded her shadow. The blessing of the Anu'enue, the Great Rainbow, was upon her. She fell to the ground and lay there, stunned.

* * *

Pueo felt her body become light. She felt herself soar and sensed a change in her perception of objects below. Fear came upon her, and darkness took the place of the soaring. She faced the fear and slowly, steadily, challenged it. She became aware that if she focused on the darkness, it would engulf her with a seductive strength. In knowing that, she moved toward the soaring sensation and discovered, with a cold shudder, that she was in flight over the Haleakala Crater.

Her first reaction was to hesitate. But she knew this flight was due to the blessing of the Anu'enue, and she shook herself free of the alarm she felt and began to fly. Her vision was uncanny. She scanned the detail of the barren cinder-covered landscape beneath her and she swiveled her head to the right and saw the white feathered wings that carried her, the wings of a great owl. She found that she could flap the wings three or four times and soar without further motion for minutes with only minor corrections in the wingtip feathers.

The air was cool in the morning sun, and no hot air thermals were rising from the crater floor right at that moment, so she trimmed up the wing feathers and glided across the crater and down the Koolau Gap.

A swift motion caught her eye when a dash of brown and gray flashed in front of her. She recognized the swept wings and darting flight were those of the kolea, the golden plover. The bird turned in graceful flight and came into formation under her. It appeared to be unafraid and sought refuge under her talons. The kolea grew in stature until it overshadowed her presence, flipped over, and then flew above her in the sky. As the kolea flew, Pueo felt great pleasure, and then great pain and loss. She banked to look up, only to find the kolea was gone.

Quickly, she searched the ground beneath her, but all she could see was a large thatched house on the side of the mountain. She sensed that people were inside of it, crying to be released, but a dark tree held the house within its limbs and roots. From the forest burst an immense brown boar that charged the house. As Pueo watched, its tusks tore the tree from the side of the house, uprooted it, and cast it far into the sea. Emerging from the house, the people were angry with the boar instead of being grateful and began to stone it, whereupon the boar ran up the side of the mountain, transformed into a kolea, and flew away into the northern sea.

Pueo flew after the golden plover, but she could not keep up with the swift bird. Reluctantly, she flew back to the mountain from which she had come. Flying up on the air currents that had now become warm, she soon became aware of another owl flying alongside her. She turned and looked into its golden flecked eyes and immediately the darkness overtook her.

She found herself awakening from the deep sleep upon the Pohaku Palaha stone. In the moments that preceded her awakening, she became aware that she had stared into the eyes of death, and that she would look into them once again in the future.

* * *

Pueo stretched, picked up her net bag and calabash, and began to walk up the ridge toward Hanakauhi Mountain. Before her, clouds rolled up the windward Maui slopes and struck the hot wind rising from the crater. As if by magic, the clouds dissipated into nothing. She wondered why the old ones had named the mountain "cloud maker," when it seemed the opposite. She chuckled and said aloud, "Cloud *eater* would be more appropriate."

The old woman stared down the Kaupo Gap. The valley before her drained toward the south and the island of Hawai'i. On the other end, the Koolau Gap drained the seven-mile crater to the northeast, and in between, the volcanic valley was covered with cinder cones and lava flows.

Pele, the volcano goddess, had been at work recently, and from the side of the ridge Pueo was walking on came steam from the hot lava that had poured down several months before, effectively blocking the Kaupo Gap to foot travel. The rugged route she was on would be the only route open for travel until the lava cooled some more. Pueo wound her way down the face of the ridge, trying to keep away from the poisonous gases. The big rocks, blown out by the last eruption, made her passage difficult and lent a mystical presence to what was already a surreal landscape.

Near the center of the crater, Pueo stopped at a strange collection of rocks. Nearly hidden from view was a large hole in the ground. Cinders funneled into the hole, and a careless person could easily slide into the pit from its edge. One outcropping of lava rock stuck out over the pit and Pueo climbed it, knelt on its top, and unwrapped a ti leaf package from her net bag. "I have brought you something to eat, Pele," she said into the air.

Silence.

"Here is some pork with salt and a red fish." The silence continued. "Here is some poi and taro leaves to go with the pork."

Pueo heard a rustling and shuffling behind her. When she turned, she was not surprised to see a gaunt white dog. Its ribs showed through the skin on its sides, and it growled a little and withdrew when she tried to pet it. Pueo laid the food out on a ti leaf and climbed down from the rocks, setting the food on the ground. The dog approached, eyeing her with suspicion before it sniffed at the food.

The dog circled the food and then, beginning with the pork, ate all of the food, carefully licking every morsel left on the leaf. Pueo took the lid from her calabash and poured water from the gourd into the lid. The dog came to her, without hesitation now, and eagerly lapped at the water. When it had finished, it cocked its head to one side, bared its teeth in a wicked grin, and loped off in the direction from which Pueo had come. As she watched, the dog ran into the grasses around the rocks she had bypassed a half hour previously and disappeared.

The climb out of the crater was an arduous one. Of the two possible routes, she chose the slippery sands. As she struggled along the path, Pueo recalled the many trips she had made into the crater with her teacher. The woman had made her climb out on all of the difficult routes. She had explained that if Pueo could climb the difficult cliffs in life, plumbing the depths of her soul would come easier. Besides, the goose hunters and sweet potato farmers used the other trail and Pueo wished to remain inconspicuous. She climbed nearly three thousand feet, ending up at Kilohana two miles above sea level. When she finally arrived, she was almost instantly chilled as the wind gusted. Pueo gathered her cape around her shoulders and sat in one of the old stone shelters built and left on the slope by ancient travelers. She ate some food from her basket and drank some of her water. Looking at her dusty legs and feet, she noticed that the sandals were nearly worn through. The lauhala sandals, good for two or three weeks at Kaupo, had survived only one trip through Haleakala. Pueo replaced them with the spares she had stored in her basket and stuffed the old ones back inside as a reminder to weave some more when she got back to sea level where the pandanus grew.

After spending the night in the travelers' cave, she left at first light. The walk down the northwestern slope of Haleakala was pleasant and uneventful. Pueo saw the yellow blooms on the mamane, and watched the tiny amakihi wing its way through the brush, alighting now and then to sing and then fly on.

She walked through the koa forest and into the grasslands and sweet potato fields of Kula and Makawao. That evening she found a safe place to sleep, ate some of the food she still had left, and slept until dawn. By the next afternoon she had reached the ponds at Kanaha, and when evening came, she had arrived at her destination at Waiehu.

CHAPTER 3

"UUUII!"

The greeting rang out in the front of the grass house. A voice replied, "Come in, come in and eat."

Pueo entered the house, set down her net bag and calabash, and stood peering into the darkness. "Pueo, is it you?" came the voice.

"Yes, Waahia, it is I."

"Auwe!" the voice exclaimed. "Come over here and let me see you."

The person behind the voice became visible as Pueo's eyes adjusted to the darkness. Waahia was twenty years older than Pueo. The older woman's stooped body bore the scars of spear fights as well as the ravages of age. But transcending the evidence of age was a cascade of white hair that fell softly to her waist.

"It has been a long time, my teacher," Pueo said.

"Yes, Pueo, but I have been expecting you. Come and sit and eat. You must have had a difficult journey."

"It was nothing, my teacher. To see you again makes the journey worthwhile." Pueo knelt in front of the woven mat and embraced her. The older woman called out, and a young girl, obviously a novice dancer, came into the house and bowed before her. "Bring some water so my guest may wash herself, and then we will eat," said the teacher.

The young girl backed out of the house and returned shortly with a large wooden calabash filled with water. Resting against the side was a dipper, the bowl of which was made from a coconut. The girl washed Pueo's hands, arms, and legs, and gave her some water with which to wash the dust from her face. Pueo smiled as she remembered having washed guests in the same house on many occasions when she herself was a girl.

Then the novice brought a cool bowl filled with poi and green breadfruit that had been baked in a ground oven and cooled. There was in addition some duck, cooked with the breadfruit, and a little salt with red clay mixed in. The meal was completed with a pinch of kukui nut relish.

Pueo ate her fill and thanked the older woman. In gratitude, from her bag she pulled several sweet potatoes she had carried from near her home, well-formed and fresh. Waahia's eyes lit up. "Ahh," she said, "You have brought my favorites. There are no finer sweet potatoes than those from Kaupo."

Then from a small package in her bag Pueo pulled several stones. They were heavy for their size and slightly elongated in shape. They had been hand polished with a great deal of work. She presented them to the older woman.

Waahia held them between her fingers and clacked them together rhythmically. The stones gave a loud *click* as they were hit together in a tempo of an old hula ili.

The old woman asked, "Where did you get these marvelous stones?"

"I found the rock," Pueo replied. "Ko'i fashioned them with his hands."

"Thank him for me," Waahia said. "How is your blind warrior?"

"He is as good as can be," Pueo replied. "His hands get stronger as he works with his weapons and he keeps himself in condition with exercises and mock-fighting."

The older woman nodded. "Yes," she said. "I would hate to be his opponent. The elderly say that the blind have unusual powers of hearing and smell, and can develop sight without the use of their eyes. He has strength as well." Pueo nodded.

The two women had fulfilled the required etiquette. Food had been offered and accepted. Gifts brought by the traveler had been praised and accepted. The small talk of friends had been made. Pueo got down to business. She addressed her teacher in the formal manner. "How did you know I was coming, kumu?"

"Your owl has been visiting me lately," the old woman answered. "She sits upon my house in the evening, and I dream frequently of a pueo owl and of a great presence to come."

The teacher continued, "I have often considered our relationship, Pueo Luahine, and I have known that someday you would surpass me as a prophetess. Perhaps that time has come, for I am older than I have ever expected to be. I counted seventy bloomings of the ohia lehua flower, and now I require a staff to assist me when I walk. Have you come to help your king as I have done? Or is your mission of another nature?"

Pueo considered before speaking. Then she bent and placed her forehead on the ground in front of her teacher. "Kumu," she said, "I am not worthy to walk across the stones you have tread upon. All I know you have taught me."

She straightened back up and continued. "A gift of sight has been given me. I have seen this presence of which you speak. I have come to seek a child."

"Your own?" asked the elder.

"No, kumu, I seek a child born twelve moons ago to a woman of the island of Molokai. The mother is of a great royal line, and the father of the child is not known."

Waahia looked at Pueo for a long time. "And you, Pueo, do you know who the father of the child is?"

"Yes, kumu," the younger woman answered, "that was given to me in a dream. The name is—"

"Do not mention the name," warned the older woman, holding up her hand.

"Pueo," Waahia said, "you carry within you the blood of the great Pa'ao, the progenitor of the priesthood of these islands. Were you a man, you would be a great priest, or perhaps a priest warrior of the old style."

She rested a moment before she went on. "Because you are a woman, certain things have been denied you. You may not eat pork, certain fish, or bananas. You must eat only with women. But you are high born within the priesthood, and your rank ennobles you with certain prerogatives. You may sit with the highest kings of these islands. You are welcome at any place of worship. The people provide you with food if you so desire."

The older woman breathed deeply and stared at Pueo before she spoke again. "But with your privileged status and the knowledge I have given you come a responsibility that an ordinary person cannot know." The old eyes stared deep into Pueo's younger ones. "Within you is the knowledge of the rise and fall of kings; the deaths of thousands of humans; the burning of canoes and houses; rape and pillage and sorrow. You must not sow these seeds irresponsibly. You must not!"

The teacher was breathing heavily by now. "Come in the morning, to the heiau temple, and pray with me. In the morning, we will go to find the bastard child."

* * *

The temple was on a hill above the stream that drained Iao Valley. Huge stones had been piled on top of the hill and they made up an elaborate complex of buildings, stone platforms, and walls. Within the walls rested the gods of the ancient people, wooden images of Lono, Ku, and Kane, as well as the lesser gods.

A special room was kept for the war god of the present king. It had been hidden from view since the Maui king's defeat at Hana two years before. There were apartments for royal visitors. These made up a line of small grass houses with stone bases, and included some quarters for resident priests. The complex was guarded by lesser chiefs and their soldiers.

One of those soldiers, a twenty-year-old man of Wailuku, was on duty at the entrance as the two women walked slowly up the hill. Waahia was well known and respected by the guards and priests of this heiau. The younger-looking companion who helped the old woman was unknown to him. Being a foolish and self-important young man, he decided to challenge the women.

"Halt! What woman dares to enter the confines of this holy place wearing a cape?" He stepped between Waahia and Pueo, his light javelin held across his body.

Pueo looked the soldier in the eye and without hesitation grabbed the spear, tripped the man with a quick twist and ended up standing over him with one foot between his legs, holding the javelin point at his throat. With her left hand she swept aside her cape. Between her breasts hung a palaoa, a symbol of power carved from a whale tooth, suspended from a braid woven from the hair of her ancestors. In the old manner of derision, Pueo extended her tongue in mimic of the palaoa's shape, then called out the name of her ancestors for the soldier to hear. When she had sufficiently cowed the foolish youngster, she stepped back and heaved the javelin. It flew through the air before it lodged, quivering, in the trunk of a coconut tree.

A priest who had watched the commotion came forward. "The owl woman makes little of our soldiers," he said with a broad grin.

"The spurs of this rooster are in his mouth," Pueo replied. The two women and the priest laughed as the mortified soldier retrieved his spear and, sufficiently embarrassed, returned to his post. Pueo walked back to him and in a low voice admonished him to train harder and to think carefully before pushing his weight around. She also told him she would keep his disgrace from his captain. The shamed soldier said nothing.

Pueo spoke briefly to the priest, and then, with her teacher, entered one of the grass buildings. Around the walls of the building were carved images made from wood. At the base of the wall stood stone figures that were worn badly but were of great antiquity.

The two women knelt in the center of the floor, on woven mats, and began to chant. Waahia began by calling out the name of a god, and Pueo would chant the history of that god and thank him for blessings received. Then she chanted praises to the god and promised fealty to him.

The chanting went into the night, and in the middle of the night, it ended. Exhausted, the two women slept on the mats within the house of one of the priests and were cooled by the trade winds coming across the hill from East Maui.

CHAPTER 4

IN THE MORNING, the wind blew in gales. A storm that dumped rain on Huelo and Haiku swept across the sandy isthmus of Central Maui and scattered sand and dust along the road upon which the two women walked. Rain began to fall and quieted the swirling dust as the winds abated. The women's travel took them a short way to Wailuku, where they found a row of houses on a bluff overlooking the ocean.

"We will visit Aalaonaona, the fragrant one," said Waahia. "She is a great beauty. Because of her high rank, the king has provided her with a house and some retainers, but as a landless chieftess, her chances of marriage are slim."

The old woman walked slowly, leaning on her intricately carved staff. "Aala has been fearful for the life of her child," she explained. "It is rumored that one of high birth is the father, and some of those in line to succeed the king would like to see the child dead."

Pueo, who had matched her faster gait to that of the older woman, asked, "What is the child's name?"

"She named him Kihauui," replied the older woman. "But she calls him Kolea."

Pueo stopped in her tracks and gave the older woman a searching look. "How did he come by that name?"

"On the day of the child's birth, a plover with black plumage on its chest flew to the beach where Aala was giving birth and strutted around the woman while she was in labor."

The two walked to the house at the end of the line. They were admitted and found Aala alone with her child. Waahia introduced Pueo to the young woman. "This is Pueo Luahine from Kaupo," she said. "She would like to talk to you about your child. I will go outside and leave you alone." The old woman limped outside and pulled the kapa curtain closed behind her, leaving Pueo alone with Aala and the boy.

"I have come for Kolea," Pueo said.

Aala glanced at her sharply. "What do you know of my child?"

Pueo answered, "I know of his parentage, and I know also he has many enemies. Those enemies would see him dead before his time."

Aala began to weep. "How did you find these things out?"

"It has been given to me to see the future, and I have been told to take the child and raise him in seclusion," Pueo answered.

Through her tears, the younger woman asked, "Can you tell me of my future?"

"No," said Pueo. "My vision is only of the boy, and that must remain with me. If you are careful, you will live to see him again."

"If I give him to you, when will that be?"

"When he comes to you of his free will," answered Pueo. "But he will be told of his parentage when he becomes a man and he can defend himself."

"Can you tell me of my son's future?" asked the younger woman.

"Only this," replied Pueo. "If he lives to adulthood, his children and their descendants will count his name first when they chant their genealogies."

Aala drew in her breath, and finally, she nodded. "This child was born of great passion. He was conceived in the cave of Laamaomao, the wind god of Molokai, during the darkest night of the fall moon of Hilihehu," she said. "I have known someone would come for him. You must take him away without the king's court knowing of his whereabouts, and you must protect him with your life."

With that, Aala wrapped her child in a kapa, and handed him to Pueo.

Holding the child against her breast, Pueo joined Waahia outside and walked back to Waiehu. The two women heard the sobs behind them but hurried on. They did not see the eyes peering at them from within the darkness of one of the houses in the row.

Back at the house of Waahia, Pueo ate a meal, fed the child, and gave him an herb to induce sleep. With many thanks to her teacher, she departed with the child disguised as a package in her net bag. She walked to the houses of the fishermen and looked for someone who would take her to Kaupo in his canoe. One man had his canoe prepared for such a voyage, and he stepped forward. Pueo haggled the price with him, and when an agreement was reached, she entered the canoe and helped paddle it out past the reef.

The fisherman stepped his short mast, and set the plaited lauhala sail onto the wind toward Kahului and East Maui. Pueo contented herself with making the child as comfortable as possible as the canoe dipped up and down in the choppy seas, making certain the child was still hidden and sleeping in her bag. The fisherman steered with his paddle held tightly against the lee side of the canoe, and they made excellent time down the coast.

Finally, Pueo fell asleep. Her sleep was troubled by the constant tacking and coming about, but at last the canoe cleared Kahului and began a long tack outside the reefs of Paia.

She dreamed that the canoe was drifting without steerage and awakened to the realization that indeed it was. As if in a dream, she found herself grappling with the fisherman, who was armed with a pahoa. He slashed at her with the sharp stone dagger and cut the arm she had thrown up to defend herself. As he slashed at her, she reached her leg behind the fisherman and shoved on the elbow that had just passed her face, causing him to lose his balance on the shifting canoe.

Pueo's quick reactions saved her. The fisherman lost his advantage and fell onto the iako arm from which the outrigger was suspended. Frantically, he grasped at it and held on as his body went into the water and the canoe careened about without steerage. Calmly, Pueo reached into her net bag and withdrew the weapon Ko'i had crafted for her. The handle was a small grip made of kauila wood. Where a blade would have been was a thin shaft of the hard wood embedded with eight small sharks' teeth.

Reaching behind the canoe arm, she grabbed the man by the hair and yanked him toward the side of the canoe. She wrapped his hair around the canoe arm and held the knife at the fisherman's throat. "Tell me who put you up to this and I will spare your life," she said. "Keep silent, and I will spill your blood in the ocean."

"It was Mahi, the son of the king," the man cried as he thrashed and fought against her. Pueo pulled the dagger closer to his neck. "I swear it, I swear it!"

Letting go of his hair, Pueo slashed a mark across the man's forearm in the same place he had wounded her. "See how fast the treacherous servants of Mahi can swim," she shouted as the fisherman let go and was left behind in the choppy waters. "The sharks may have a good supper." And then, as the man splashed toward shore, she grabbed up the paddle, plunged it alongside the canoe, and brought it back on course.

* * *

The child finally awakened from his deep sleep as the canoe rounded Opana Point. Pueo had navigated the canoe well out to sea, and her next tack became a long reach that carried the fisherman's canoe along the coast of Maui's windward shore.

She lashed the big steering paddle to the side of the canoe and fed the boy some poi. The change of caregiver did not seem to bother the child, as Hawai'ian children were often shuffled from house to house and grew up with surrogate parents. The kings and queens often gave their children to other chiefs to raise, away from the intrigue of the courts.

Keeping well away from the dangerous cliffs, Pueo guided the little canoe past Keanae. She came closer to the shore and dropped the woven sail. Paddling from the stern, she managed to bring the canoe through the mild surf and into the mouth of a small stream.

It was nearly dark when she got the canoe lashed to some trees at water's edge. She found some bananas and fed the child the fruit, poi, and a little dried fish that she chewed for him.

That done, Pueo slept in the canoe with the child, and before the break of day, she was paddling out through the surf, setting sail, and reaching around Nanualele Point past Hana. Again, she steered the little canoe well out to sea. It would not be wise, she knew, to come too close to the Hana district and its occupation army.

As she tacked onto the wind off Hana, the canoe began to gather speed. The outrigger skimmed the water and Pueo felt a wild exhilaration. In the sky above flew the iwa. The dark bird soared in an effortless flight, its forked tail stretched out behind. The weather was all she could ask for, and after she had passed Hana and the fortress of Kauiki, she took the sail down and fished with the bone hooks and coconut sennet she found in the stern.

The current and wind carried them along toward Kaupo, and in the meantime she played games with the child She caught an ahi, and knew that Ko'i would be pleased with the little tuna. Her hook was taken next by a big fish, and she took fifteen minutes to hand line it. Seeing the sun dropping in the western sky, she brought in her lines, stepped the little mast, and sailed into Kaupo.

Some fishermen along the shore helped Pueo pull the canoe up above the rocky beach. They admired the canoe, for it was well made, and asked her how she had come by it. She replied that she had bought it in order to take Ko'i fishing during good weather. The fisherman saw that she had the boy with her, and they nodded when she explained that her sister had given her a child because she and Ko'i had no offspring of their own.

She then cut the big fish in pieces, gave some to each of the three men and thanked them for helping her. As the sun began to set, she tied the child in front of her with a piece of kapa, slung her net bag in back of her, and began the long trek up to her ledge.

Pueo stopped halfway up the hill, and fed the child some more banana, poi, and fish. She completed her journey in darkness, placing her feet by memory as she climbed through the forest.

Ko'i heard her coming long before she arrived, and he stoked up the cook fire in anticipation that she had brought something fresh. "*Uuii!*" she called out as she came down the hidden path to their ledge.

She was happy to see that he was waiting for her. "Come! Come!" he said. "Come and eat. I have some poi and some cooked breadfruit." He stood to embrace her and sensed a hesitation on her part.

"I promised to bring you something," she said, "and I have kept my promise." Pueo handed him the sleeping child.

He took the child and was astounded. "What is this!" he exclaimed.

"It is our son. You will raise him as your own, and someday he will be a fighter, the equal of Koa Ko'i," Pueo said.

The big man stood trembling with the child in his arms, unable to reply. How often he had dreamed of a son, but he and Pueo could never conceive one of their own. Stroking the child's head, he fell to his knees.

Pueo continued. "You must never ask me of his parentage. That will be revealed to you in time. You and I will raise the child as our own."

"What is his name?" asked Ko'i.

"His name," she said, "is Kolea."

CHAPTER 5

DURING MOST OF THE YEAR, Kaupo has a warm, semi-arid climate. The trade winds travel across Hana and Kipahulu, dropping rain on the upper slopes and valleys, which are some of the wettest in the world. Perennial streams of water wash down the slopes and cross the dry, fertile coastal plain.

For centuries, the people of these districts cultivated fields of sweet potatoes, and in the wetter areas, taro. These staple foods are both nutritious and easily digested and eaten together with fish, seaweed, and other products of the sea, they were responsible for the healthy and robust population.

The presence of the rich fields had also been responsible for envy. For as long as the storytellers could remember, the chiefs of the island of Hawai'i had been trying to wrest the Hana, Kipahulu, and Kaupo districts from the kings of Maui. Sometimes they succeeded, but usually, the highly respected fighters of Maui had hurled the invaders back into the ocean.

During the time of Pueo, Ko'i, and Kolea, the Hawai'i soldiers controlled only a small toehold on Maui, but it was a stronghold as well. The fortress of Kauiki was the key to control of the Hana district. It consisted of a small crater in the top of a cinder cone hundreds of feet above the bay. Its steep cinder slopes were wooded and provided cover for the soldiers who guarded the secure outpost. At the top were stone works from which the warriors within could hurl spears and stones at their attackers below. The fortress could be reached and supplied from the sea, and it lacked only one amenity: a steady supply of water.

During the ten years since Pueo had brought Kolea to Kaupo, the king of Maui had invaded Hana twice. Each time the preparations, sacrifices, and training had been to no avail. The Hawai'i soldiers had simply backed into their redoubt and, from there, launched devastating attacks on the king's troops.

The king's only son and heir apparent, Mahi, had become a war chief of no small reputation. But his reputation was stained by a cruel streak that manifested itself in many ways. He was fond of disfiguring the bodies of his enemies and making use of their bones for such degrading materials as fishhooks and arrowheads for shooting rats.

Mahi also had other evil inclinations. Wherever his troops went, parents of young women were certain to send the girls to relatives in other districts. Mahi made it a habit to procure the most attractive in the district, and his private sessions were rumored to be of a depraved nature. His father, King Nanoa, was disgusted with his son's personal life, but because of his military abilities, he tolerated them.

Mahi had just suffered a defeat at Hana. He was marching his troops through Kaupo and on to Kamaio when he heard the story of the Owl Woman and the adopted child who lived in the mountains. Mahi dispatched five warriors into the hills to search for the boy. He then settled in, ordered some girls brought in for his pleasure, and awaited the capture of the owl woman and her ward.

Three of the searchers went from farmstead to farmstead inquiring after the pair, but no one would give the information they sought. The other two warriors, wiser in the ways of seeking information, bribed a local man and, after getting what they wanted, headed directly up the mountain to the hidden ledge. They walked quietly through the forest, following the trail described by their informant and noting the signs of travel that had been well hidden.

The trail became indistinct at a point where it neared the cliff's edge and, after consulting quietly, they began a search of the area.

Before long, one of the searchers rediscovered the trail and the two crept down the narrow pathway.

The steep path wove through large rock outcroppings and narrowed to a point where the men were required to go through single file. The narrow place opened out onto a ledge forty feet from cliff face to edge, more than one hundred feet long. To the right were two thatched houses, and in front of the houses knelt a small woman.

The two soldiers harrumphed and walked up to Pueo. "Where is the boy," the bolder of the two barked. She looked up and instantly recognized the soldier she had humiliated years before at the temple in Waiehu. He recognized her as well, and with a sneer he cocked his spear arm at her.

But Pueo was not afraid. "Who seeks him?" she inquired.

"That is not for you to ask," the soldier answered triumphantly. "We will ask the questions."

The two soldiers heard a noise behind them and turned toward one of the houses. The sound was that of a boy chanting. The spokesman walked to the house and shouldered aside the woven door. Crouching to get under the door beams, the two entered the house with their spear points leading the way.

Inside the darkened house the warriors discovered an eleven-year-old boy seated before a small drum chanting an ancient mele. The two soldiers stood inside the door, looked around, and walked toward the boy.

At that moment they considered their mission accomplished. But there was one flaw in their thinking. Their informant was chuckling over a piece of information he had withheld from them: Ko'i.

Crouched in the darkness, Koi smelled the two warriors. His acute hearing told him they stood shoulder to shoulder. Although it had been ten years since his last battle, his senses were honed to a fine edge. In a blur, the blind warrior struck. Inside the house he disdained all weapons except his hands and feet. Grabbing each soldier by his outer ear, he drove their heads together with a resounding *thud* and then, wrapping his great arms around their necks from behind, he squeezed until both necks broke.

He and the boy dragged the two bodies out to the edge and pushed them off the cliff to the barren rocks below. Pueo chanted a chant of death and of respect for the two soldiers, and she cast ti leaves over the cliff after their bodies. Then she sprinkled salt water on the boy and Ko'i.

"We must leave this place," she told Ko'i.

"I know," he replied. "We shall go after the darkness descends."

Ko'i gathered his tools and hand weapons into a woven sack. Kolea carried a supply of dried fish and poi, and Pueo folded her kapa and placed some loaded calabashes into her net bag. The three ate in silence and then hiked down the trail to Kaupo. They kept to the trees, avoiding the open roads, with Kolea leading Ko'i as he always did when they went fishing.

As they neared the village, they came upon a heavily guarded house and heard shrieks and a great commotion coming from inside. Pueo whispered to Ko'i and separated from the two males as they approached the house. Ko'i, hidden in the trees, held the boy to his side in the shadows as a nude girl covered with bruises ran from the door. She was pursued by a man perhaps a foot taller than Ko'i. The blind warrior stiffened and drew the boy closer to him as the laughing man, assisted by his guards, dragged the screaming woman back into the house.

The boy began to cry and huddle closer to Ko'i as he led the blind man down the road toward the canoe landing. "Why did we have to stand there, Ko'i?" the boy asked.

"It is wise for you to look into the eyes of your enemy," he replied.

The pair walked down the cliff overlooking the canoe landing and paused when they heard the low-pitched whistle. They carried their bundles toward the sound and sat down in the darkness near the roots of a hala tree.

Pueo spoke quietly. "The landing is heavily guarded. Mahi is taking no chances." Looking to Kolea, she said, "When you see the light from the outer canoes, take Ko'i to ours and get it in the water. Paddle out fast to the point, and wait for me there."

Kolea nodded and watched as she removed her clothing, packed it in her bag, and handed it to Ko'i, who carried the extra weight with ease. In a moment Pueo was gone without a sound.

Ko'i and Kolea waited. Five minutes passed and then another five. They heard the guards murmuring to one another beneath the cliff. Kolea sensed something behind him and started to turn, but found his mouth covered with a huge hand that held him in a viselike grip—it was Ko'i, keeping him quiet, for two guards had approached them from the rear.

Ko'i, with his acute sense of hearing, had spotted them long before the boy had. The blind warrior relaxed his grip on the boy and carefully prepared himself for an attack. The boy sat still as Ko'i had instructed him. The guards, still searching methodically, were quartering the area and narrowing it down.

One walked so close that Kolea could see the tattoos on his arm. The guard stopped, as if sensing the two, and turned toward the shadow where they hid, beckoning his compatriot with a hand signal. Kolea saw the knuckles on Ko'i's hands turn white as he gripped the shaft of his dagger.

Boom! Boom! Boom! The boy almost leaped into the air. A signal drum was sounding nearby. Both guards abruptly turned and ran toward the outer point. Kolea saw a big double canoe on fire on the beach. Quickly, he searched the area below him for other guards and finding none, he led Ko'i down the familiar path to their canoe shed. Dumping their packages into the canoe, they got under the outrigger arms and lifted.

Ko'i picked the front up and carried the canoe, dragging the stern and the boy behind him out of the shed and into the surf. The canoe, blackened with pa'ele paint, was nearly invisible in the darkness, and as Kolea scrambled into the rear of the canoe, Ko'i kept walking until only his head showed above the surf. With an agility not common to most men of his size even with sight, Ko'i leapt into the canoe, grabbed a paddle, and silently paddled through the surf.

As Pueo had instructed them, they waited off the point, and before long Kolea spotted the flashing eyes and teeth of the woman as she swam through the water toward the canoe. Slipping silently onto the canoe, she moved the boy into the center of the canoe, picked up her paddle, and together they paddled away from the bay and Kaupo.

The three voyagers paddled to sea in the canoe. The hull was old, but sound. Ko'i had insisted on rubbing the hull with a mixture of black ashes and kukui nut oil every time he and Kolea had used it to go fishing. He had kept the canoe in a stone shed with a thatched roof and had replaced the sennet, which held the gunwale strakes to the dugout body, wherever they had become worn.

The maintenance had paid off well as the canoe creaked and groaned through the long swells off the southeast coast of Maui. They paddled steadily, saving their energy when they could, and let the current carry them past the bay. As the dawn colored the sky over the hills at Lualailua, they turned their canoe into the sheltered lagoon of Molokini Island.

CHAPTER 6

THE TINY ISLAND consisted of a half-cinder cone that rose out of the sea in the great volcanic rift zone that comes out of the ocean at Hana, marches up the volcanic mass of East Maui, through the Haleakala Crater, and down the eastern slope of that mountain to the shore at Makena and beyond. The three travelers searched the shore for sea bird hunters and finally, weary from a night's travel, pulled the canoe onto the beach and rested. At dawn, Kolea and Pueo took turns watching from the top of the little island.

When it was Kolea's turn, the boy climbed the sandy hill to keep watch while Pueo slept. He was an awkward-looking boy. Other children often teased him about his large ears, and he had grown his thick black hair long in order to cover what he considered a gross defect. The long hair also covered a large head that, like his hands and feet, were out of proportion to his body. Thick eyebrows jutted out over a handsome flattened nose and moderately thick lips.

Sea birds flew out of their nesting burrows and dived at him, and he knew there would be fresh eggs for the evening's meal. Keeping a wary eye on the sea around him, Kolea searched the burrows. Warding off the diving birds with one hand, he brought the eggs out one at a time, checking them for freshness. As Pueo had taught him, he returned the eggs with developing embryos to their burrows and took six fresh eggs for their meal that evening.

Hiding the eggs from the sun, Kolea began to forage along the shoreline. Try as he might, he was unable to capture the delicious black rock crabs that skittered in and out of the rocks. After an hour of pursuit, he gave up and gathered several fresh limpets instead. The little opihi were plentiful on the windward side of this island.

He was carrying his bounty back up the hill when he noticed the sail out on the water. In his preoccupation with food gathering, he had forgotten what he was there for. The sail jutted skyward like the giant claw of a crab. He could tell the canoe was a large double and it was headed directly toward him.

Kolea scrambled up the hill and down into the crater that half surrounded the lagoon. "Ko'i! Pueo!" he shouted.

The sleeping pair awakened quickly, and Pueo climbed the hill with the boy. She was surprised to see that the canoe was only three miles off and running before the wind. As it was, she estimated that it would require only about ten minutes for the canoe to reach the tiny island. She saw the boy fumbling to pick the eggs up and shouted, "Get Ko'i and put the canoe to sea. Stay close to shore and watch me for instructions. Leave the eggs."

Kolea ran down the hill and saw that Ko'i had already launched the canoe. The boy jumped in and together they paddled out of the tiny bay and around the island. Kolea watched Pueo. She scrambled around the top of the island just out of sight of the big war canoe, motioning to the boy to paddle on or to stop. Kolea told Ko'i about the signals, and the blind man laughed loudly as if it were all in a game.

The big double canoe, paddled by fifteen men in each hull, rounded the island. A man standing on the deck shaded his eyes and peered into the cove they had just vacated. Seeing nothing, he gave orders, and with sail and paddles, the war canoe was once again under way, headed toward Kahoolawe Island.

Pueo watched until the canoe was gone around the south end of Kahoolawe and then came down the hill and beckoned the little canoe into shore. "It looks as if we will travel in the night again," she said. She noticed that Ko'i was still laughing, and she too began to laugh, at first quietly and then with loud peals. Soon all three were on the warm beach holding each other and whooping with laughter at the fine game they had just played.

In penance for his inattention, Kolea volunteered to keep the afternoon watch. Taking a small plaited mat for a sunshade, he spent half of the day on the hill, looking out.

With time to think, Kolea wondered why the two men had come for him the night before. He knew that there was some mystery in his past, but he had not thought much about it, since his days had been filled with schooling, play, and helping Ko'i with his weapons. Pueo was a stern teacher and required much of him, but he also detected respect from her, which made him her equal rather than a mere student. Even Ko'i, when no one was looking, would carry him around on his broad shoulders the way the chief's children were carried in public.

The boy remembered the tales Ko'i had told him of battles he had fought. He had begun to take instruction in the formal chants as well. Pueo would chant, and the boy would repeat each stanza until she was satisfied that each syllable and each nuance was correct. Although he was too young for formal warrior training, Ko'i had taught him about weapons as they sat on their haunches and worked the wood and stone parts.

He enjoyed the hard work with Ko'i. They would sit for hours at a time, working the wood. First with the stone knives, Ko'i would rough the handle or shaft out of a solid piece of wood. Kolea, as his apprentice, was responsible for keeping the tools sharpened, and he would sit near the big man's feet honing the stone tools to a fine edge.

Later, Ko'i used pieces of coral to smooth the wooden parts. Next, fine pieces of cinder would be rubbed on to finish the piece. Then came the polishing. The two would rub the weapons with kukui oil until the wood turned dark and mellow under their hands. After they were done, Ko'i would frequently stand and thrust and parry an imaginary foe with the unfinished weapon. If, after swinging the weapon around for a while, he was not satisfied with its feel, he would work off a little wood here or there and try again. At that point, if the spear or club felt wrong, Ko'i would scowl and heave the defective weapon far out into the canyon below them.

Now, Kolea spent the afternoon watching the sea and wondering what was in store for them. After dark the three travelers took the canoe to sea and paddled along the Kihei coast.

They picked up a good wind coming down the mountain and sailed the canoe past Lahaina. Whales were resting in the night, and they could hear the gentle blowing from the giant creatures as they glided along. Kolea slept.

CHAPTER 7

Molokai

THE CANOE TOSSED around in the turbulent seas. Kolea had thrown up until his stomach was empty, and then thrown up some more. He felt as if his stomach would come out of its own accord. But after a while, he fell asleep in the bottom of the canoe while his two companions navigated the craft through the channel separating Maui from Molokai.

Kolea awoke to the sounds of sea birds. The canoe was under sail and traveling at a fast pace around the little island that jutted out from Molokai's east end. The birds dove at the boat and, at the last possible moment, swooped past them and back into the air. The sun was coming up, and Kolea could see that Pueo and Ko'i were worn out. The night passage had been rough in the small canoe. Ko'i stroked his paddle down into the water, but it was an automatic motion and not the joyous dipping and pulling Kolea remembered from their earlier days of fishing.

Passing around the point behind the island, they came before the wind and sailed around into a curved bay with a large stream running down into it. Steep hills and cliffs rose up on every side, and they could see many houses. Ko'i pulled the canoe out onto the sand, and a family pulling its own canoe down to the water helped bring the outrigger canoe up onto high ground.

The local chief's name was Iaea. It was obvious from the many scars on his face and upper body that he was a warrior. His district was one of the wealthiest on the island and had never been successfully invaded during his tenure. Kolea noticed that Iaea's nose was turned to one side and had a big lump on the bridge between his closely set eyes, both due no doubt to a skirmish or two. But the man's eyes sparkled with interest when the three were ushered up to his compound to see him.

The chief greeted them all, but his eyes never left the blind face of Ko'i. "So," he exclaimed. "This is the axe soldier from Maui. I have heard many tales of you, Ko'i." The chief stood up and walked around the blind warrior. "What brings you to Halawa?"

"We seek a place to live," Ko'i replied.

"My spies tell me as much. And what does that ill-disciplined pup Mahi have against you," Iaea asked as he turned his eyes on Pueo and Kolea.

"I do not know, my chief," Ko'i answered.

At that, Iaea sounded a little surprised. "You address me as 'my chief'?"

Ko'i paused, and Kolea watched the tired muscles of his back twitch slightly. "Give me your hand, Iaea."

The chief stepped forward with a smile of anticipation on his face. He placed his right foot next to Ko'i's extended foot and gripped his right hand with that of Ko'i. The two stood as if carved from wood for several seconds. The muscles of their backs and arms were bunched and straining as if bound tightly by cords.

Ko'i leaned forward slightly and gripped until the perspiration beaded on his forehead. And then slowly but inexorably, Iaea began to bend. He resisted, as if a great weight was on his shoulders, but he was forced to his knees by the strength of the blind man. "Lawa!" he yelled. "Enough!"

Kolea did not know what to make of what happened next. In his brief experience, he had been led to believe that it was kapu to touch a chief except in battle. But here was this great war-chief jumping up and down laughing and slapping Ko'i on the back with his good hand while swinging the other hand around his head in obvious pain.

"You are welcome here, indeed," Iaea yelled. "Auwe! My hand is killing me. Aiiii, you have the grip of a shark's jaw. Auwe, auuuuuwe!"

And with that last yell of pain he good-naturedly dragged a bewildered Ko'i into his eating house and ordered that Pueo and Kolea be cared for and given quarters befitting Pueo's status as a dancer.

Inside, Iaea seated Ko'i on a lauhala mat and had some poi and fish brought in. The two men ate in silence, and when they had finished, Iaea spoke. "I do not know what Mahi has against you, but my spies came back from Maui last night with the information that he is in a great rage because you slipped through his net."

Ko'i could not see the other man but could tell that Iaea was enjoying the telling of the story. "They say that two of Mahi's best soldiers were found at the base of a cliff in Kaupo, and that one of his big double canoes was found burning on the beach."

At this Ko'i still said nothing, and Iaea went on, obviously relishing the tale. "I think what embarrasses him most is the fact that a blind man, an old woman, and a young boy did the whole thing."

With this, Iaea lay back and roared with laughter. Ko'i could hear him rolling around on the mats, cackling with glee. When Iaea could contain himself once more, he sat up again, blew his nose in a cloth, and went on. "He believes that the owl woman made you invisible. Is this thing possible?"

Ko'i thought about this for a while and then spoke. "My chief," he said, "with Pueo anything is possible. But one thing I know. She is better at starting fires than she is at making others invisible."

Iaea began to laugh again, and when he had finished, he said, "Axe soldier, I would have you train my son in the arts of war. You may take refuge here in any case, but I would be honored to have you take over the education of my son."

Ko'i nodded. "I am preparing to begin my own son's training, and perhaps Kolea can grow to be a soldier in service to the great Iaea, or his descendant."

"Perhaps," the chief answered.

* * *

Iaea's son was called Makanunui. His name described him well: big eyes. Among Iaea's three wives, Makanunui was the only boy child. No matter how much he was urged to eat, Makanunui remained a slender boy, though taller than average.

With his dark skin he resembled no more than a brown piece of rope. The slender form was always in motion. When his father wished him to be taking instruction in the stones, Makanunui would be down helping the taro farmers shunt water from one irrigation system to another. By the age of twelve, he had a detailed knowledge of the operation of the water systems, which irrigated hundreds of patches in Halawa Valley.

If his father was searching for him in the taro patches in order to send him to his tutor of genealogy, the boy would be at the beach hopping from foot to foot as he watched the warriors lash hulls and outriggers into a sea-going unit. He helped weave nets, fall trees, catch birds, prepare fish, and climb for coconuts. But he disregarded and escaped from everything his father wanted him to do. Until he met Ko'i.

Here was a man of skill, the boy discovered. Kolea, who accompanied him everywhere, held no particular interest for Makanunui. But when he saw the intricate handwork in the spears, axes, and knives produced by Ko'i, he immediately wanted to learn from the blind man. Ko'i offered the boy a deal. If he would take instruction in the stones with Kolea, Ko'i would take Makanunui as an apprentice.

An apprenticeship for a chief's son was highly irregular, but then Iaea was a highly irregular chief. Lacking the great legions of warriors commanded by the chiefs of Hawai'i and Maui, Iaea lived by his wits. His fame was built around lightning attacks by small well-trained bands of soldiers who hit and ran, living off the land as they fought. He had a thousand surprises for his opponents.

When Ko'i told him of the deal, he nodded and agreed immediately. Iaea knew that there were many trails to the top of a mountain. Besides, he took a secret pride in the notoriety his son was achieving. And now, with the training that the blind warrior and Ko'i's son would give him, in five or six years, the boy would take his rightful place as a soldier.

And so Makanunui began to work with Ko'i and Kolea. During the mornings they would go with Ko'i and climb the trail to the grassy area above the red dirt cliffs where huge stones stuck out of the sides of the cliffs like fruit ready to fall from a tree. Makanunui, to his delight, found that when he and Kolea were not leading Ko'i, Kolea could walk as fast as he could. In fact, the strange-looking boy was not only a fast walker but had an unerring sense of the trails. From years of guiding the blind man, he had learned to trek up hill and down via the easiest route, avoiding the dangerous cliffs and gullies as if by instinct.

On their first day, when they had reached the top of the hill, Ko'i had the boys locate a flat upright stone. This they did quickly: the grassy area was littered with large stones as if a giant had strewn them about in a marble game. Ko'i had the boys gather dozens of stones of the size that they could hold in their closed hands. Then he took a packet of moist red dye from his bag and marked a two-foot circle on the stone at chest height. Ko'i walked off sixteen paces, and then marked an area on the ground with the stick he carried. From that area, he stood, blind eyes facing the target he could not see.

"Bring me a stone the size of my fist," he told Kolea. When the boy had done so, he stood relaxed, facing the stone. With a motion almost too fast to see, he heaved the stone. It struck the center of the target with a resounding *whack* and shattered into eight pieces that fell to the ground, much to Makanunui's amazement. "When you can do that," the blind man said, "we will begin with the small spear. Do not throw more than fifty of the small stones today. You are working on speed and accuracy, not strength."

Ko'i sat and listened while the boys threw their rocks. From time to time he would comment, "Too slow," or "Not enough follow-through" or "Point your hand directly at the target as you release."

When the boys had finished, Ko'i made them gather more stones and throw left handed. Neither boy was able to hit the target with any authority. And when they did, it was with a tiny *plink* as the trajectory was too high. "Hah!" Ko'i yelled. "What happens if you have a wound in your right arm? Do you give up? Run away? Work on your left arm until it excels in the battle with your right. After all, it has fewer bad habits."

The boys worked on the stones until each had thrown their quota. Then, sitting cross-legged with the blind man, they listened as he taught.

"The throwing spear is a deceptive weapon. You can do great damage to your enemy when you throw it, but you can only throw it once. Therefore, you must practice for the one throw. A single throw can turn the tide of great battles. When you can throw the stones well, I will teach you the spear. When you are expert with throwing, we will get Iaea to teach you his art."

"What is that?" asked Kolea.

Ko'i rocked back on his haunches and said, "Iaea is the best spear-catcher in these islands. I have heard of him catching four thrown spears during a combat and sending them back at his enemies in such a rapid manner that two of them were struck down before they could do anything."

Makanunui fidgeted and said, "Ko'i, you promised to teach me to make weapons."

"So I did," the blind warrior said. And with that the man pulled some items from his bag. There were pieces of cord made from olona fibers.

"Slingshots!" Makanunui's exclamation covered his disappointment poorly.

"Ah," Ko'i said, "have you one already?"

"Of course," the slender boy answered.

Kolea remained silent, knowing what was coming.

"Sling a stone at the target rock," Ko'i said.

"That's easy," the boy replied. "I herd the pigs back into their pens with my slingshot." And so saying, the boy leaped to his feet, picked up a stone, swung the loaded sling around his head and let fly. The stone snapped through the air and struck the target with a loud *crack*.

"That was fine," said Ko'i. "Now watch Kolea."

Kolea stood self-consciously, loaded his sling, whirled in around his head and released it. A noise akin to the hum of a bee caused the hair to stand up on Makanunui's neck. In the split second the stone was in flight, the sound rose to a loud buzz, the stone struck the target with a *whack*, twice as loud as Makanunui's had, and disintegrated into so much powder.

The chief's son stood, his mouth agape in shock.

Ko'i laughed. "Sit down, Makanunui, and we will begin to build the fine weapons you desire." The blind man felt in his bag and pulled out several stones. Shaped like fat spindles with longitudinal grooves, they were perfectly symmetrical, tapering to a point at each end. "These are my own invention," he said as he handed some stones to Makanunui.

"But they are of soft stone," said Makanunui, digging his thumb-nail into the side of the stone.

Kolea explained, "Ko'i makes them of soft stone on purpose. They carve out easily and spread out damage on impact more than the hard stones do."

The blind warrior followed up by telling the boys what the unusual noise did to enemies. "You must not be simply strong in battle," he instructed. "Your battles are sometimes over before they start. An opponent who is afraid before the battle begins can often be caused to run away by simple acts that he cannot understand."

"You mean like loud noises?" Makanunui asked.

"That is one method. But let me warn you of one thing," Ko'i continued. "You may scare away the doubters, but you must always be prepared to be close, face to face, and hand to hand with the good fighter, for he will not run."

"Never?" asked Kolea."

"*Never!*"

CHAPTER 8

IT HAD BEEN FIVE YEARS since Kolea and his adopted parents had come to Molokai. One night, Ko'i lay awake thinking about his students. Kolea was the stoic one. He sat and listened, and did the exercises required of him, but did not speak much. The incident on Molokini when they had fled from Mahi had not been characteristic of the boy. He almost never forgot what he was told.

There was something else Ko'i had noticed. Kolea had an indefinable sense about him. It manifested itself in the forest where Kolea could walk silently and blend in with the sounds. Had Ko'i been able to see, he would have noticed that Kolea blended visually as well. Ko'i relished the trips into the forest with the boys. Kolea would stop them and imitate the sounds made by birds. Soon, birds would flock into their area and fly around the three, singing and answering the boy's noises.

Kolea would tell Ko'i how the birds looked, what they ate, and how they moved around. The boy's interest went also to the plants of the rainforest, and he could go alone into the woods and bring back herbs for Pueo and materials for Ko'i's weapons.

Most of all, the boy was patient. Ko'i knew that the fierceness needed to be a great warrior would not come until the boy developed some emotions. But for the most part, he was satisfied. If Kolea could learn to fight, he would be a powerful warrior someday.

While others flew around like birds strutting and posturing, Kolea would make the hard decisions. He had sense.

Makanunui—now, Makanunui was different. Where Kolea was patient, Makanunui would jump around like a flea and talk in a voice so rapid that Ko'i would become exasperated trying to understand him. Where Kolea would practice with the sling stones to become accurate, Makanunui would spend his time experimenting with the spindle-shaped stones until they made fierce shrieking sounds such as Ko'i had never before heard. The boy was always experimenting with the weapons and tools, but he made up for his impatience with one trait he had in common with Ko'i: he was a perfectionist.

Once when Ko'i was manufacturing a stone axe, Makanunui sat next to him, grinding tool edges and working on a tool of his own. When Ko'i had tied the head down tightly with many fine lashings, he stood and swung it about his head, changing hands frequently and feeling its balance. Makanunui spoke to him, "Try mine, Ko'i."

The old soldier put down his axe and grasped the proffered weapon in his hand. The finish was somewhat rough, but the balance was superb. Ko'i swung it about him in a mock fight and then passed it back to the boy. "I have felt axes made by so-called experts that would not have equaled this. Where did you learn to do this?"

"From watching you," Makanunui answered. "That is my first axe."

From that day, Ko'i had taken the boy seriously. They worked together, and Ko'i was pleased to sense no jealousy between the two boys. Each admired what the other was good at, and they had become inseparable.

Early one morning the two boys, carrying slingshots and bags, were off to the east coast of Molokai to hunt birds. The two were an unlikely looking pair: Makanunui, tall and dark with long muscles in his legs and a stride that covered the ground quickly, and Kolea, now sixteen years old, had grown larger but was still an awkward-looking boy.

"Come, Kolea, you walk like a poi dog," Makanunui teased.

"Ho," cried the younger, "I have not the legs of a stilt such as you have."

The boys climbed the trail as the sun came up. "I have a feeling we will see many birds today" said Kolea. "Perhaps the nene will be back on the rocky area east of the grassland."

"If so, we will eat goose tonight."

At the top of the twisting two-mile trail, the boys paused to look around. From this point, below the sacred kukui grove, they could see the rolling hills of grass that went toward the south coast two miles away. Eager to hunt, they loped along, watching the golden light ripple in the long grass. The boys passed the sweet potato fields where Iaea kept a small outpost to warn him in the event of an overland sneak attack. Their minds were far from war, and they could spare no time to check through with the men on duty.

For the boys, it turned out to be a fortunate oversight.

They swam in the early calm near the rocks and, with some wooden spears, captured some manini. The little black and white striped fishes were sliced and eaten raw, and the remainder carried on a twig. Then the boys worked their way up the hill toward a dry area of grass and rocky lava. Geese used this area for nesting, and the boys had learned to sneak quietly through the lava field and sling their stones at the geese from hiding places in the rocks.

Makanunui teased Kolea often, but when the boys hunted, he ceased the teasing. Try as he might, he could not emulate Kolea's stealth. The awkward boy passed through brush and grass as if only a small breeze was passing. Makanunui crouched as the other boy did, and watched him cock his head to listen.

Suddenly, Kolea turned to him and placed his hand over his mouth to indicate silence. Kolea appeared to be listening to something, but Makanunui couldn't hear it. Kolea motioned him down, and they pressed their ears to the smooth lava at their feet. To Makanunui, it was a strange rumbling sound. To Kolea, however, it was unmistakable—the sound of many marching feet.

The two boys scrambled to a vantage point and looked down to the coast. Along the coast trail, stretched out for more than a quarter mile, came a column of warriors. At the lead, carrying a spear, was a middle-aged chief. The boys could see that the chief's cape was brilliant yellow with a red diamond in the center. He wore a woven helmet with the tufted crest of the island of Hawai'i.

Kolea counted the men. "There are more than a hundred," he said.
"We must warn my father," Makanunui said.
"They will see us in the open," Kolea said. "Follow me."
Makanunui ran after him up the small gully where they had
been hunting. At the top, the boys traversed the lava bed and began
to crawl through the tall grass toward the outpost.

When they were out of sight of the oncoming troops, they leaped
to their feet and sprinted up the slope through sweet potato patches
to the outpost. Makanunui got there first and burst in.

As Kolea, breathing heavily, ran up to the house, he saw his
friend backing out with a bewildered look on his face. Peering into
the darkness, he could see the soldiers asleep on the floor. Food and
drink were spilled all over the floor. Kolea leaped up to one of the
soldiers and shook him violently. "They are drugged!" he shouted.
"The Hawai'ian army must have been here!"

Makanunui nodded. "Listen to me, for we must act quickly."
After giving instructions to Kolea, the slender boy raced down the
trail to warn the village. Kolea began to climb the slope that led to
the red cliff above. On the top of the cliff was the sacred kukui grove.
Pueo had taken him to the grove when she had special chants to
perform, and he had often played along the cliff tops while she was
thus occupied.

Stopping near the trees, Kolea took the time to leave a small
offering of fish on the flat stone near the grove entrance and then he
picked up a large stick to take with him to the station Makanunui
had assigned him.

He was not a moment too soon. From his hiding place at the cliff
top he could see Makanunui running down the trail. Looking back,
Kolea saw the Hawai'i soldiers coming around the sweet potato
patch he had recently crossed.

Kolea could see a man come out of hiding near the outpost. The
man was gesturing wildly toward the trail where Makanunui was
running. The soldiers of Hawai'i seemed not to pay attention to the
man at first, instead pulling the drugged outpost soldiers into the
road and murdering them right then and there. Kolea did not turn
away at the sight of bloodshed, but within his breast rose an emo-
tion he had not known before. Controlled anger took over.

Grabbing the big stick he had hidden behind the rock, he began to dig. The stone was eight times his size, and from the side of the red dirt cliff, it jutted up like a great thumb. The boys had often speculated through the years about when this balanced rock would fall. Shoving the dirt to one side, Kolea dug until the stone was just balanced on its edge. Then he waited.

The troops were hurrying now, nearly to the top of the trail. Makanunui was racing down the last two hundred yards into the village, and as he reached the first buildings, he shouted a call to arms. The call was repeated, and soon a conch shell sounded.

With all chance of surprise lost, the Hawai'i troops began to hurry down the trail. They kept silent to keep those below from guessing their numbers. Suddenly, a shrieking noise echoed above them, and the men stopped. It was an eerie sound, and several soldiers looked about for hiding places.

The chief in front urged them on, but another shrieking sound swept over them, and many made signs against the unknown evil. In the confusion, the troops bunched up into a group, and it was then that Kolea dug the remainder of the dirt out from under the stone.

At long last, the stone began to tip—and then it paused. Kolea shoved out more dirt from below, but nothing happened. Swiftly, he slung another of Makanunui's stones out over the troops below, and then, grabbing the great stick, he jumped above the stone, drove the stick down behind it, and levered it over its fulcrum.

With a cloud of red dust, the stone began to topple. Ever so slowly at first, it lay flat and slid. Picking up speed, it reached the brush line and struck a larger rock. Now the stone flipped end for end and began to crash down through the brush faster and faster, gaining speed as it traveled downhill.

As Makanunui had expected, the troops panicked. They ran in all directions, but mostly downhill, falling over one another in their haste. Some warriors dropped their weapons. At the bottom, they were met by the troops Iaea had mustered.

It was no contest. Many of the Hawai'i troops were killed in the skirmish, and others surrendered in fear of the unknown horrors above. Kolea jogged back to the trailhead. As he passed the flat offering stone, he saw that the fish was gone. High in the trees, eating the fish and watching him, sat an owl, and he knew they had been protected.

The two boys were heroes. A feast was held and the Hawai'i chief was sacrificed at the war heiau. Iaea appropriated the canoes that the Hawai'i warriors had hidden near their landing site. The other canoes were divided among the soldiers of Molokai. A small canoe was given to Makanunui and Kolea, and an old man named Ho'okelo was assigned to teach the boys navigation.

CHAPTER 9

THE LESSONS TOOK place along the windward cliffs of Molokai. Ho'okelo had the boys paddle up and down the coast and impressed upon them the dangers of a lee shore. These were heady days: riding the great swells up high into the air so they could see the rocks a hundred yards away and then running down into the trough where only the cliff top showed above the water. In the next two years, the boys developed powerful shoulders and arms and were impressed by the sea's power.

Ho'okelo would blindfold each boy and make him lie in the bottom of the canoe and learn to give directions by the feel of the waves as they met the canoe's hull and outrigger. The old man told them that if they learned the regular patterns of swells, they could navigate at night without danger.

One day the two boys walked to the shore and found Pueo helping Ho'okelo with preparations. With her she had several bundles of supplies and containers of water. "Where are we going?" Makanunui asked.

"On a journey," she said. "You have learned to crawl, and now you must walk." Confused, the boys helped launch the canoe, got in, and paddled out of the bay.

Now in their late teens, the boys had become young men, though they were still boys at heart. Makanunui was tall. He had a wide forehead with tightly curled black hair. His eyes were very dark, and they darted about, noticing everything, as if they were storing knowledge for their owner. He was still slender, but his back and shoulders had become wide and strong with the canoe paddling and spear work. He was a handsome and popular lover among the women of Halawa. He enjoyed the trips in the canoe, most of all when they encountered bad weather. He seemed most at home in emergency situations where his quick mind could function.

While Makanunui was tall, Kolea was even taller, dwarfing his companion. His head had fulfilled the promise of his big ears. His eyes were evenly spaced beneath a thick brow. When the young man looked at others, his gaze was steady and did not dart about. Kolea's nose was flat with flaring nostrils, and his lips were full enough to be considered sensual and desirable among the women of Halawa. His shoulders were also broad. Even when Makanunui and Kolea graduated from stone throwing to spear work, he continued to work on the stones, throwing ever-larger stones at the target until he could match some of the more seasoned adult warriors in power and accuracy. The young man's hips carried his upper body well, and his legs had grown strong from the running.

Ko'i had told Kolea that the warrior who could run for long distances had the best chance in battle, and like most of his lessons, he had accepted and worked on this knowledge. He had but one great desire: to stand as an equal among the warriors of Iaea.

The young men dipped their paddles into the water and drove the canoe forward into the long swells that came from the east. They had never been out of sight of the island, but their knowledge had been gained from listening to Pueo's chants. The chants were like astronomical charts. Pueo made verbal pictures of the heavens, and placed the constellations in perspective so the boys could tell where they were in relation to their islands by reading the stars.

Celestial navigation had been practiced by Polynesians for thousands of years, and Pueo taught Kolea the chants of those navigators. From Ho'okelo he learned of stars that lay below the southern horizon, and of the locations of seventy-three rising and setting stars by which he could set a nighttime course. He learned of the great star of gladness, Hokule'a, which Pueo told him would pass just north of the island of Oahu in its nightly pursuit of the sun.

In addition to the star points related by Pueo, the boys had learned other arts of practical navigation from Ho'okelo. His grandfather had made a round-trip voyage to Tahiti fifty years before, and he had passed his gleaned knowledge to Ho'okelo. Together with his local knowledge, this voyaging information made him a reliable navigator.

On this day, Makanunui and Kolea paddled for several hours, resting occasionally to drift in the big swells. To the north of Molokai was open ocean, no choppy channel winds or buffeting shoreside gusts to complicate their progress. Soon they had paddled far enough so that only the very tops of the mountains showed above the horizon. Here, in the afternoon sun, the water was deep and a dark blue. When the last tip of land winked at them from beneath the tops of the swells, Ho'okelo instructed the young men to set the sail.

Kolea set the mast in its socket, and Makanunui tied the lines that stayed the mast and the curved boom to the outrigger arms. The canoe leaped forward and Ho'okelo set a course toward the east. The navigation master marveled at the turn of speed this ordinary-looking canoe made.

Only the rudiments of the canoe had been given to Makanunui. Ho'okelo had watched him finish the work, eyes gleaming on it as if it were a favorite toy. The young man had gauged the hull thickness, and then spent many days scraping the canoe with sharp stones and pieces of coral. He would remove a little in one location and then scrape some from another place. He had redesigned the outrigger so it was more buoyant and sliced through the water more quickly.

After he had altered the canoe to his satisfaction, Makanunui had polished it to a high gloss with kukui oil and black ash and finished the hull with a cloth made from the skin of a young shark. He and Kolea had won many wagers with their canoe.

Now, rocking and sailing across the wind, they were glad of the four people and the ballast they carried. Their canoe was wonderful for paddling and running on the wind, but the weight gave it stability on this tiresome rolling motion. During the night, the boys took turns keeping watch on the steering paddle.

In the early light of morning, Makanunui spotted some birds sitting well above the water, and the young men paddled over to have a look. The birds were perched on the bare branches and roots of a great floating tree. The tree was bigger than any tree growing on Molokai.

Ho'okelo said, "Kanaloa has sent us a tree. People from Kauai have told me of these logs floating in from the sea. They make long canoes from them."

Makanunui climbed onto the log with a sharpened stick and probed the wood. "It seems sound, "he said. Kolea paddled their canoe on the lee side of the log, picked up Makanunui, and followed the wind, current, and waves back to Molokai. Once there, Makanunui examined the shore and appeared to be making one of his calculations in his head, and they took the canoe along the shore and back to Halawa.

CHAPTER 10

A STORM CAME IN that night and blew hard for three days and nights. On the morning it subsided, Makanunui and Kolea left before dawn and paddled up the coast. They found the tree near where Makanunui had predicted it would come ashore. Huge waves had blown the tree above the shore and lodged it in the bushes. Kolea kept the canoe off the shore while Makanunui swam in and inspected the tree. He had never seen anything like it. The giant spruce log, which they judged had floated from a faraway place of which they were unfamiliar, was over a hundred and fifty feet long and carried its girth well up into its crown. He probed it with a small stone knife, and then swam back to the canoe. "We need to bring Kahuna kalai wa'a here to check this and see if it can be our wa'a."

After paddling back to Halawa, the boys consulted the kahuna who, as the chief canoe builder, was also the last word on whether a log was suitable for carving into a hull. The old man gathered some belongings and food, and they paddled him back to the log. When they had deposited him on the shore, he told them to come back in two days. As they left they saw him placing his ear against the timber.

The next morning Kolea followed Makanunui to the forest behind Halawa. Makanunui dug up a parcel he had hidden. Kolea asked, "Why is Kahuna kalai wa'a spending two days for this task?"

The answer was slow in coming. "He is talking to the tree and listening to its answers. He will tell me if it contains a canoe. He will know if hidden insects have weakened the tree and whether it was split inside where we can't see it. He usually stays one night with a standing tree, but this one came from the sea and is different. So he is staying with it two nights." At that, Kolea nodded and they started back from the forest.

Back in the village, Makanunui led them to the house of Uulani. The woman was large and had the quick strong hands of a weaver. She was plaiting pandanus leaves that had been divided into long strips. The lauhala mats she wove were as fine as any Kolea had seen. Makanunui told Uulani that someday he would build a fine voyaging canoe and would need sets of woven mats for sails.

At that, Uulani scoffed at him and turned to Kolea. "Will he do it, or is this just another boast from a chief's son?" Kolea looked her in the eye and said, "He always makes good on his promises. I will go to Tahiti with him."

"We shall see," Uulani said, and went back to her plaiting.

The boys did not see the young woman, Uulani's daughter, watching them from inside the house.

On the following day the young men paddled down the coast to find the kahuna. He was sleeping next to the log and awoke when he heard them pulling the canoe ashore. "What do you think of the tree?" asked an anxious Makanunui. He wanted to build a great canoe and no one in Halawa had seen a log this big, he knew.

The old man replied, "The tree is sound and it has the strength to be a great canoe. My question to you is, do you have the perseverance to bring the spirit within this tree out where it belongs? If not, your father will find a canoe builder who will give this tree the second life it deserves." Makanunui figured that there would have to be a discussion with his father about this, and so the boys and the kahuna paddled back to Halawa.

In the evening, the boys, accompanied by the kahuna, joined a circle of men outside Iaea's house. Two canoe builders were there along with Ko'i. "It is time to find out whether all this jumping around from one thing to another has formed Makanunui into a man of competence," his father said.

Iaea asked one of the builders to examine Makanunui. The builder began by asking a question about seagoing design. Makanunui stood and brought forth a thin sharpened stick and began to draw in the dirt. He quickly sketched the outer design of a fifty-five foot double-hulled canoe. It was unlike any they had seen, with modified wave-breaking bows. The builders pored over the design and nodded. "It is not like our designs, but it should work if constructed well," they informed the chief.

"What is your experience with the tools?" asked another man. This question brought a smile to Ko'i's face. Kolea watched in amazement as Makanunui opened the packets the boys had carried from the forest and laid out several shining stone adz and axe heads and some handles and hafts to be fitted. Each tool was polished to a mirror finish on the cutting edge, and the canoe builders picked them up and handled each one. "Where did you get these?" asked one of the men.

Ko'i answered. "He made them himself. Makanunui took my designs and made them better." After a short discussion the canoe builders told Iaea, "This boy is capable of designing a canoe, and we saw the job he did in improving the captured boat. Only time will tell if he has the tenacity to stay with it on a canoe of this size."

The next morning the boys, along with the Kahuna kalai wa'a, paddled back to the big tree and waited while prayers and blessings were given by the kahuna. Then they began by chopping off the stubs of limbs remaining from the tree's long time at sea.

In two days the three had cut the huge tree into two sixty-five foot logs and had placed small logs as ramps perpendicular to the tree and rolled the big logs into the sea. Other, younger boys from the village brought canoes, tied lines onto the logs, and towed them to Halawa, where the small logs were placed on the beach and the two big logs hauled up to the Halau wa'a canoe shed.

Makanunui began to rough out the bottom of the canoe with the adz and chips began to fly. Unlike the red-brown of the koa wood the boys had worked with on other canoes, this tree's wood was white, even-grained, and easier to work with the stone tools. In the beginning, the work was slow going and the kahuna was there giving advice and stopping the work when he saw some problem that the boys could avoid. "Take care," he would say. "There is no other log, so slow down and get the bottom right." He counseled the boys to find the direction the chips came out with the least effort, and to use the adz in that direction. "Work with the tree and the tree will cooperate with you," he said. Other boys came to help, and Makanunui trained some in tool making so they could keep the stone tools sharpened and swap them with the dulled tools on a frequent basis.

The bottom of the canoe had the rounded shape of the large canoes in use in Hawai'i, and the bottom tapered from the center to both ends so the sea could lift the canoe evenly from the bow or the stern. They left a bit more wood in the stern, so the canoe would track well in a seaway.

Weeks and then months went by, and Kolea and Makanunui became more efficient at the work. They developed muscles they did not know they had. At one point they began to use the finishing adz with its wider blade to smooth the outside of the first hull. Slowly, bit by bit, the log began to look like a canoe.

Their growing experience made the work on the second hull go easier. Each evening was spent sharpening the tools for the next day's work and, after consuming huge meals, the young men slept well.

During the work, Makanunui and Iaea commissioned Uulani and her daughter Haunani to begin plaiting two sets of sails for the canoe. Several women in the village joined in the work, and for a while, the sail making became the gossip center of Halawa. The older women freely discussed the personal anatomy of the two boat builders amidst much hilarity.

The quietest worker at these gatherings was Uulani's daughter Haunani, who smiled and listened to the chatter while her hands flew across the lauhala strips, weaving them into the huge crab-claw shaped sails.

Haunani was a tall girl with broad shoulders, long glossy black hair, and the strong hands of a weaver. She was widely desired by the boys and men of Halawa but gave off signals that said she was not available. In a society where sexual activities were encouraged within certain bounds, she was unusual. But her mother was a powerful force in the community and told her she should do as she wished.

On days she was not weaving, Haunani watched the boys going through their fighting exercises and later copied them, working out in the forest where she could not be seen. Pueo noticed her activities and befriended the girl. Each morning after Pueo had chanted and danced the sun up out of the ocean and Kolea had left for his work, Pueo would spend an hour talking with Haunani and teaching her the healing and the defensive fighting arts she was so good at. After several months, Haunani became accomplished at using the short spear, and her quickness with the weapon surprised Pueo.

By then, Molokai had been at peace for a long time. While Iaea kept his defenses ready, it was a time for growing food, teaching children, repairing houses and canoes, and drying fish.

Meanwhile, the canoe hulls had been turned over and Kahuna kalai wa'a instructed the boys to carve the insides in only one direction. "Follow the grain of this log," he said. "It is not like our trees. It asks to go forward in the sea and fights off your tools if you don't work with it."

Most of the finishing work on the twin hulls was done by Makanunui. Kolea spent his time hewing the upper sideboards out of koa wood and drilling the holes necessary to lash them onto the dugouts. Under Makanunui's tutelage, the younger boys carved the iako arms that would join the two hulls and provide a base for the platform where voyagers would live. The mast and the boom had been carved to fit the great sail Uulani and Haunani had plaited.

CHAPTER 11

A FULL YEAR HAD PASSED since the boys had found the great log and the village had worked on the canoe built from it. Now, the canoe was effectively finished, and they were putting the final touches on it.

Makanunui had added weight and developed muscles. He could work hard and efficiently for long hours. Kolea grew broader in the chest and shoulders, and continued his early morning runs up the steep trails of the valley. His hands grew very powerful, and during their daily hour of instruction with Ko'i, he showed his instructor that someday he would become a fearsome opponent in battle. Iaea told the boys that they must continue warrior training while building the boat, so each morning they would take lessons from Ko'i.

"I will show you how a lua fighter works his magic," the blind warrior said. "Grasp your little fingers together." When the men had locked fingers, Ko'i told them to pull. Back and forth they pulled until Makanunui gave in and ran about shaking his hand and howling. "You are at a disadvantage," Ko'i told him.

Kolea had begun his training with Ko'i before coming to Molokai. A lua fighter learns to accept pain and isolate it in a separate part of his body, he had been told from an early age. A lua fighter shields his fighting ability and keeps a clear head. "Give me your hand," Ko'i said. Makanunui did so and Ko'i pressed on certain nerves in Makanunui's arm and, as if by magic, the pain disappeared.

"Fighting is half of the lua fighter's ability," Ko'i said. "Healing and adjusting wounds is the other half." And so the blind warrior taught them the Hawai'ian healing arts.

There were ways to relieve pain. There were herbal concoctions to promote the healing of wounds. During the training, a man was brought to Ko'i with a dislocated shoulder, and the blind warrior sat on the ground, placed his foot in the man's armpit, and reset the dislocated shoulder back in its socket. He told Kolea and Makanunui that a warrior's life required balance, and that every damaging thing that was done required an offsetting act of good in order for a man to truly be a warrior.

Ko'i taught grappling techniques and how to dislocate each joint from fingertip to shoulder. He showed them bone-breaking locations and how to use ordinary objects as weapons. Kolea became expert at a dozen striking blows that could disable an opponent.

And then Ko'i produced a thin cord with a short stick woven into one end. "You may use this object to choke a person and to kill him. But it must be in combat and not as a revenge or criminal act."

After a month of grappling training, Kolea asked when he and Makanunui would take instruction with the short and long spears and the fighting axe. Ko'i answered with a question. "When you are paddling the king's canoe in battle, do you paddle with a spear?"

"No" they replied. "That would be foolish."

"That's right," the blind warrior said. "When an enemy attacks from their canoe, the weapon you have is the weapon in your hands." With that, Ko'i brought out a canoe paddle and began a series of complicated exercises.

The blind warrior circled them, jabbing at them with the pointed upper shaft and dropping into a crouch while spinning and swinging the edge of the paddle at their shins, causing them to jump to evade the blade. He seemed to know where they were, even without his eyesight. After a while, Ko'i stopped, broke into laughter, and told them to bring their paddles to the next lesson.

As the two young men walked to the village, Makanunui told Kolea that some of the others had been ridiculing him for taking lessons from a blind man.

Kolea laughed and told him about Ko'i breaking the necks of the two warriors sent to kill him. He said, "If you asked any man in this village to fight Ko'i without weapons, only the foolish would do so. They would find out about his uncanny abilities. He sees without eyes and can follow you with his hearing, his sense of smell, and the small air currents that come from your movements. Before anyone is stirring in the morning, Ko'i is out lifting stones and doing a set of exercises that loosen and strengthen his muscles."

Early the next morning, Makanunui went to the clearing where Ko'i and Kolea exercised and began to work. He stretched, lifted stones, and copied their movements.

During the weeks and months that followed, a change in the instruction took place. Ko'i, recognizing the seriousness of the two, moved their training into a different phase. The canoe paddle became an extension of the body, and the design of the paddle for the dual purpose of paddling and fighting became an obsession with Makanunui. He worked certain woods that had flexibility and sheer strength and brought them to Ko'i for approval.

The two were taught by Ko'i to use the war axe judiciously. "Wild swinging is useless and wastes the energy needed for a long battle," he instructed. "Keep the axe close and strike hard at the time your opponent is least expecting your attack. If you have no axe and your opponent comes swinging one, close within his swing and grapple with him. He cannot do damage to you with his swinging axe if you are gripping his body up close."

Ko'i began the spear training with the short spear. "Your father will be your instructor in throwing the long spear. He is a master," he told Makanunui.

Kolea took to the short spear. His strength and speed gave him an advantage, and during the sparring periods he could usually get the edge on Makanunui. But on occasion, Makanunui would trick him with feints he had learned from watching Ko'i and plant his spear behind Kolea's leg and push him to the ground. At that, Ko'i would laugh. "Strength and guile are two brothers. Alone, they are good. But together, they are excellent. Each of you must learn from the other and when in a fight stay together and baffle your enemies." And so they did.

CHAPTER 12

ONE DAY WHILE Kolea and Makanunui were rubbing pumice on the hulls to prepare them for the finish, Haunani banged on one side of a hull to get their attention. When the men came around, they found her carrying a huge bundle of sennet. She handed it to Kolea and told him, "My mother said it was time to begin lashing the strakes to the dugout."

Makanunui pulled a strand of the small rope and said, "This is very strong. Your mother is really good at this."

"She is, but I made this," Haunani said. She looked into Kolea's eyes and added, "I made all of this." And then she walked away.

Kolea put the bundle down and began to coil the strands in big loops. He reached inside the bundle and pulled out a short piece of bamboo. "What's this?" he asked Makanunui. He had never seen anything like it before.

The other man glanced at the thing and smiled. "It's a nose flute. She made it for you."

Kolea looked puzzled. "Why?" he said. "I don't know how to play it."

Makanunui broke into such laughter, he fell to the ground and rolled back and forth until he could regain control. He stood, and with tears of laughter running down his face he told his friend, "Well, you'd better hurry up and learn."

As the two were putting the tools away, Makanunui told the still-puzzled Kolea, "You are spending so much time with these tools, you are ignoring the one you were born with." And with much laughter and head shaking, Makanunui walked away, saying no more.

Kolea finished coiling the rope and headed home. When he got there he found Pueo crouched by a small fire, cooking fish for their dinner. She looked up at him. "Where did you get the nose flute?" she asked.

"Haunani gave it to me," he replied.

The old dancer nodded. "I wondered who the lucky one would be, "she said.

"What do you mean?" Kolea asked.

Pueo shook her head. "Come and eat," she said. "After dinner, we will try to penetrate that hard head of yours."

Kolea and Ko'i sat together and ate baked breadfruit, poi, and the manini fish Pueo had prepared on thin sticks. They could hear Pueo muttering from her eating place on the other side of the grass house.

"What's all this about?" Kolea asked him. Ko'i, having heard the earlier conversation, shook his head and just laughed. "Don't ask me. I am the kumu of weapons. She is the kumu of everything else."

After the meal, Pueo and Kolea climbed the trail up to a bluff that overlooked the sea. They sat on a flat rock and there, Pueo instructed Kolea in playing the nose flute. He pressed a forefinger against one nostril and exhaled through the other until he could coax a steady note. Pueo showed him how to finger the notes and let him practice for a time. The sound was pathetic, but she let it go on for a while. Then she stopped him and asked him to relate his experience with women.

Kolea admitted that he was without experience, and that his entire love life had been conducted in private and alone. "Women approach me," he said," but I am not comfortable just jumping into the bushes with them. I thought someday I would find someone who was more than just a passing whim."

Pueo looked him in the eyes. "Well, it appears that someone has found you," she said.

"I like Haunani, but I don't know how all of this goes about," Kolea said. So for the next two hours, he took instruction in issues of the heart and other organs of both men and women. Each evening he would climb the trail. Out of the hearing range of the village, he practiced on the flute until he could produce a clear set of haunting notes that, according to Pueo, he had to compose himself. It was the plaintive call of a lover.

One night, while the village slept, Haunani was awakened by the sound of the nose flute in the forest behind her home. It was as if a bird sang a soft song and it called to her as none had ever done. Quietly, she draped a cloth around her hips and followed the sound. Through a taro patch and past a crop of ti leaves she followed the sound until at last she came to Kolea.

There he sat, cross-legged on a mat he had carried with him, and he continued to play. Without speaking, Haunani sat with him. In the darkness she reached for him and found his erection. With just a few movements of her hand Haunani caused Kolea's pent-up sexual pressure to explode.

Kolea was distraught, but Haunani whispered to him that it was expected on the first occasion. He realized that Haunani used the exact phrases used by Pueo when she had instructed him and realized that they had both been going to the same teacher. His erection did not subside, so Haunani pushed him back onto the mat, straddled him and the two of them learned other things together well into the night.

He came to work late the following day and was greeted by a smiling Makanunui. Kolea avoided his friend and worked opposite him as the lashings were being fitted to the canoe. The hulls were shiny black where Makanunui had polished them with oil from kukui nuts mixed with ash from burning lauhala.

Makanunui's voice came across the canoes. "How was it?"

"Kuli kuli oe. None of your concern!" Kolea shouted in reply. More chuckling came from the other side. When the two took a break and were snacking on dried fish Kolea asked him," How did you know what happened last night?"

"Lawe olelo—gossip. It's the common language of our people," came Makanunui's reply. "Everyone knows everything, or believes they do, as soon as it happens. Besides, that was a new tune coming from the forest. And everyone has been waiting for the only two virgins of age in all of these islands to find each other."

Kolea nodded and said, "Then everyone must know the answer to your first question. Haunani is not shy about making loud noises when she is enjoying herself." At that, the two went back to work.

After the men had lashed seven iakos across the hulls and constructed a platform from bow to stern, Makanunui consulted the kahuna. "Is it time for prayers and chanting?"

"If you have not been praying every day it won't do much good now," the kahuna replied. "But that comes when you have mounted the mast, sails, and all the rigging and other items. Launch the hulls and paddle around so I can observe the canoe in the water. Then haul it back up for the finishing touches."

The word quickly spread around the village that the canoe was finally done, and soon there were men and women helping to slide the great craft across its logs into the sea. Makanunui and Kolea each stood in a hull using ropes belayed from trees on the shore to control the ascent, and soon the canoe slipped into the water. A cheer arose from the shore as people with paddles climbed aboard.

Makanunui and Kolea assigned people to paddling positions and the kahuna, standing on the beach with Iaea, instructed the remainder to sit between the hulls on the canoe platform to give it weight. From the shore, the kahuna gestured, giving directions to paddle this way and that, to take the canoe out through the waves and to come back through the surf. Then he had the canoe left standing still in the water and turned slowly so he could see the waterlines on all sides. "What do you think?" asked Iaea.

The kahuna turned. There were tears in his eyes.

"What's wrong?" asked Iaea.

"Absolutely nothing is wrong," the kahuna replied. And he signaled the canoe back to the shore.

When the villagers had pushed and pulled the canoe back to the canoe shed, the kahuna had a pig brought. With the crowd watching he had Kolea lift the pig into the stern of the canoe. The pig ran the length of one hull and leapt from the bow, where he was captured. "This canoe will have many good voyages," the kahuna declared. "Get that pig to an imu and prepare him for his final honor." Another cheer went out and the pig was taken away for the feast.

In the evening, the roasted pig and boards covered with fish joined bowls of poi and cooked taro leaves for a luau. At the women's eating place, Pueo sat next to Haunani and the two shared a bowl of poi. "Will you go with him?" Pueo asked. The younger woman looked at Pueo. There was no question of whom they spoke. "If there is water in the sea I will go with him," she replied. "I want no life without him." Pueo nodded. "It will be very difficult. There will be trials beyond even my imagination."

"I believe you, Pueo. As Ko'i needs you, Kolea will need me. This is where my life is headed, and I am pleased with the direction."

The festivities came to an abrupt halt when a runner from one of the outposts came to Iaea. He arose and made a call to arms. A controlled chaos ensued, with warriors scrambling for their weapons and taking predetermined positions along the beach and facing the trail. Women and old men gathered children and moved them to safe places.

Soon, a small group of warriors accompanying a young chief from an outlying district came into the village. Iaea shouted out a challenge, and it was answered when the chief shouted out his name and the names of his ancestors. He then placed his spear on the ground and walked to Iaea with a small koa bowl in his hands. He handed the gift to Iaea and said, "I bring a message of peace and alliance from your friend Nanoa the king of Maui."

Iaea gave an order and his warriors stood down. "E komo mai ai. Come and eat," he said. He embraced the other man.

Food was brought to Iaea's house and the two men ate a few bites before getting to the business at hand. "You are probably aware that Hawai'i warriors have invaded the district of Hana," said the chief. "We have been unable to dislodge them so far, and my king requests the help of his friends on Molokai."

Iaea chewed on his food for a while and then replied, "We have been at peace for some time now, thanks to your king. But my warriors have kept in condition, and it is time to take the wrappings from our war god and help kick that ilio kukae back to their island. What does the king want us to do?"

The instructions were given and the young chief and his warriors headed back up the trail to visit other Molokai villages.

CHAPTER 13

THE WARRIORS GATHERED near their canoes at the beach
below Halawa. Warriors from all over Molokai were with them.
Iaea spoke. "We are joining the Maui warriors at Keanae and will
combine our forces. It will be our job to help drive the Hawai'i warriors off the Hana coast. Paddle and sail to Wailuku and then along
the coast until you reach the Keanae peninsula. Shelter on the beach
on this side and find me near the big taro patches."

Kolea and Makanunui took Kalani and Pa'akiki, two of the
younger warriors, in their canoe and paddled to sea with the fleet.
Kalani was a huge young man known for his happy disposition and
enormous strength, while Pa'akiki was very different, a small, hard
man with great knowledge of farming and the genealogy chants.

After a few miles, they were able to hoist the sail and, using the
big steering paddle to keep from sliding sideways, flew across the
wind, outdistancing many of the heavier canoes. The wind was
brisk and the water choppy, and the young sailors spent their time
bailing the water that came in over the gunwales of their craft. Kolea
broke out some packets of sweet potatoes and dried fish, and the
young men ate with gusto, knowing what lay ahead.

Along with the bright sun came malolo, the flying fish, jumping
out of the water and occasionally into the boat. Some of the small
fish were caught and eaten raw. Soon the Maui shore came into
view on their right and they headed the canoe into the shore near

Wailuku. The wind allowed them to head clockwise around Maui and as evening approached, they saw the tip of the Keanae peninsula before them. Kolea steered the canoe into a long beach as more of the fleet followed behind. After hauling the canoe up-beach, they went off in search of fresh water for the drinking gourds slung on their sides. Joining the other warriors, the young men hiked toward a bonfire the Maui king had placed as a beacon.

After the leaders had broken from their council, Iaea joined the group from Molokai. "Here is the plan," he said. "Half of us will join the king and go to Kaupo in our canoes. Tomorrow morning, Mahi will lead the other half ashore near Waianapanapa and will fight toward Hana. We will come from behind and fight through Kipahulu and put the Hawai'i warriors in a pincer. But to make this work, I have a special assignment." With that, Iaea called Kolea up to the front of the group.

"Kolea will lead a group of twelve young warriors up Keanae Valley and across Haleakala Crater into Kaupo Gap. He will cause a diversion and help us surprise the Hawai'i warriors from the sea," Iaea said. He then gathered a group of young, very fit warriors chosen for the mission and instructed them to make haste across the valleys that divide East Maui.

Kolea and Makanunui turned their canoe over to Kalani and started the group jogging up the well-traveled trail from Keanae to Haleakala Crater. He had the feeling he had been there before and kept the small patrol together. As the mountain rose before them and the air thinned out, he slowed the pace and wove his way out of the rainforest and onto the brush-covered slope.

The path became divided into a mass of pig trails, and some confusion ensued. Just then an owl flew off the slope and winged its way eastward up the side of the wide valley. Without giving it a second thought, Kolea led the group in the direction the owl had taken, and they came to an open area filled with volcanic cinders and cooled lava flows. He chose a route alongside the crater, which took them through the dry volcanic area and past the rough route.

Once through the crater, the young warriors started down the mountain, stopped at a spring near the cliffs, refilled their water gourds, and bedded down for the night.

In the darkness before sunrise they began their descent. The smooth lava flows in Kaupo Gap had cooled enough so the warriors, with their toughened feet, were able to move more quickly and soon they heard some commotion farther down in the village. Kolea realized he remembered the trail from his childhood, and he led the warriors in silence down to the outskirts of the village.

From a concealed spot they could see some Hawai'i warriors standing over a slain man. Their companions were looting the food supplies of a taro farmer.

"I will go down first," Kolea said. And when I make the bird call, come down and attack them from the rear. Make plenty of noise after you close with them." With that, he walked silently into the forest and disappeared.

Without a sound, Kolea walked up behind the two warriors. He stashed his spear in the brush and armed himself with one of Ko'i's axes. He stepped out of the trees, struck the first warrior on the side of the head, grabbed the spear from his hands, and faced the second one who was calling the alarm. Kolea made a shrill bird call. At that, other Hawai'i warriors were running toward them, shouting when the remainder of Kolea's patrol came at them from the rear and attacked.

Kolea parried the first thrust of his opponent, observed the warrior was right handed, and began to circle to the left. Suddenly, he jabbed at his opponent's face, and when the warrior raised his spear to parry the thrust, Kolea drove the sharpened rear end of the spear down into his opponent's foot. When the other man ducked in pain, Kolea finished him off with his war axe.

Meanwhile, the battle was raging in the farmer's taro patch, and Kolea's young fighters were giving the Hawai'i warriors a beating. When Kolea saw many more Hawai'i warriors running toward them, he gave a prearranged signal, and his men began to back up toward the mountain they had just descended. Kolea retrieved his spear and joined them in a controlled retreat. Once into the brush, he led his men up to an area he knew well and climbed a rock to watch.

Kolea had brought his troops up the hidden trail he had often walked as a child. When the Hawai'i soldiers gathered reinforcements and followed, they found themselves in a narrow defile heading up a steep trail into the forest. Their leader looked around them, knew they were in a weak position, and, thinking better of pursuing Kolea, turned back.

Just then, from one side, a slung stone caught the last man in his temple, and he dropped to the ground. A thrown spear, tipped with tiny shark teeth, struck the next man in the buttocks, and his scream caused the rest of the Hawai'i soldiers to run down toward Kaupo in disarray. During their absence, Iaea and the king's warriors had come ashore and taken the village, and the Hawai'i soldiers met a wall of warriors, who quickly took over the battle and defeated them. And so the battle was done.

CHAPTER 14

IAEA SURVEYED THE VILLAGE and saw that the boys had done their mission well. He embraced his son when the young troop came out of the forest. Makanunui told him of Kolea's plan and how it had worked, and Iaea took Kolea by the arm and praised him and his troop before the older warriors. Then they all joined the king's troops and began a march toward Kipahulu, pursuing small groups of Hawai'i soldiers who had been foraging in the village.

The king assigned Kolea's young men to help ferry the canoes along the shore as his army made their way toward Hana. It was slow going to windward as the boys paddled the canoes, but they kept pace with the walking warriors as the foot soldiers had to climb up and down steep gullies and fight small skirmishes along the route to Kipahulu. Late in the day the army came to the fighting and attacked the rear of the Hawai'i army, which was occupied in a battle with Mahi's warriors on the edge of the village of Hana.

Mahi was having a rough time. The best Hawai'i troops had been occupying the big village, and a hot battle was taking place. Dead and injured warriors from both sides lay in a stream, causing the water to run red. The chief of the Hawai'i warriors recognized he was flanked from the rear and backed his men down to the beach. They boarded their canoes and paddled away from the shore in a hail of spears, shouting, and stones.

As the Hawai'i canoes set sail, Kolea and his young warriors were landing the canoes on the red sand beach below the volcanic cone that had served as a redoubt for the Hawai'i troops. From Pueo's description, Kolea recognized the place as the hill where Ko'i had lost his eyes. The king of Maui ordered Kolea and Mahi to accompany him to the top to see if there were any stragglers. And it was then that a glance at the young men told a tale.

Although separated by twelve years and borne by different mothers, the two looked remarkably alike. Mahi was broader than Kolea, but the two were equal in height.

Mahi looked at Kolea and recognized him as the boy he had been pursuing for years, and then an anger took over, though he chose to say nothing just then. As the three got to the empty camp at the top of the steep cinder cone, Mahi, ignoring the king's protests, lunged at Kolea with his spear. Kolea saw what was coming and stepped to the side parrying the spear. As the spear slid alongside him, Kolea acted as Ko'i had taught him and brought the heel of his spear up, striking a blow to Mahi's head.

As blood flowed down Mahi's face and into his eyes, he spun about and blindly thrust his spear at the figure before him. His father the king, who had stepped between the two, went down with Mahi's spear in his breast and died on the spot.

Other men had followed the three to the top and came upon the trio. Mahi pointed at Kolea and said, "That man killed the king." Knowing that anything he could say would fall on deaf ears, Kolea ran down the back of the slope and into the forest. Shouting warriors chased him, but his stealth and running skills gave him a head start and he eluded them, running through the village at Hana and climbing into the forest.

As the sun set, Kolea began finding a route up the mountain. In a few minutes, he heard a familiar whistle well behind him and stopped. Makanunui had been following him. "What happened?" Makanunui asked.

Kolea frowned. "Mahi killed the king and blamed me," he answered.

"He is the new king and is sending men after you," Makanunui said. "The warriors are rounding up stragglers so they will be everywhere, and they are organizing a group to find you."

Kolea thought for a moment and said, "I can get to our canoe without being seen. Meet me at the first stream on the Kipahulu side and listen for my whistle." Makanunui nodded and began to climb back to the village.

Making almost no sound, Kolea worked his way down to the red sand beach. As he passed the village he saw a great celebration beginning as the people of Hana brought food and gifts to the Maui warriors. But at the same time, mourning had begun. The king's body was being prepared for carrying and would be taken to a secret place in Haleakala Crater and placed in the rear of a lava cave where his enemies could not find him and desecrate his bones by carving them into fish hooks.

After darkness fell, Kolea crept silently through the darkening village to the canoe landing. From the bushes, he could hear the voices of two men guarding the canoes. Many of the boats were grounded on the beach, but he recalled tying their canoe to others moored behind the larger boats. He waited until the guards were on the other end of the assemblage of canoes and then slipped into the water. Swimming underwater, Kolea found the sleek blackened sides of their canoe, pulled himself between the outrigger and the hull, and quietly slipped the rope free of its mooring. With powerful kicks of his legs as he swam, he stealthily pulled the canoe away without being noticed.

Once around the point Kolea climbed into the canoe and paddled toward Kipahulu. At the first stream he whistled and found Makanunui and two others of their small cadre waiting. Makanunui told him Mahi had beaten one of their troop and tried to find where Kolea had gone, but to no avail.

The two other warriors decided to try to get to their home on Molokai, where they knew they would be safe. Kolea nodded. In the darkness they paddled out to sea.

Using the stars and chants Pueo had taught them, the boys navigated past Kaupo, around East Maui, and by morning, they had hoisted their crab-claw sail and were making way past Lahaina and toward Molokai. They paused at a stream to fill their gourds with water and took to the channel between the islands. The wind was low in the morning, so their passage was easier than usual, and soon they arrived at Halawa.

After beaching the canoe, Makanunui asked, "What should we do?"

Kolea answered, "Go to Pueo."

* * *

The old woman was performing her morning chants. There were some Kolea had not heard before. They called on the birds for guidance. She chanted to Kolea's namesake, the golden plover, and she chanted," Ulili E, Ulili E" to the big migrating bird known as the wandering tattler and asked them all for guidance.

The boys sat respectfully until she had finished. Then Pueo turned and spoke to them.

"Kolea, you have always known that you are not the son of Ko'i and me," she said.

"I have," he said.

"In truth, you are the son of Nanoa, the king of Maui. I took you from your mother to keep you from being killed by your half-brother."

"Mahi," Kolea said.

"Yes. I know what happened on Maui. Your meeting, and fight, was inevitable, and now you must leave or be killed."

Kolea knew not to question Pueo about how she had gained her knowledge of the events on Maui. He asked, "Where can I go?"

"The birds will tell you," she answered. "Come with me."

The boys followed her to a hidden area behind the grass house. Ko'i was waiting on a stool. He rose and embraced Kolea. "You and Makanunui have learned your lessons well, or you would be dead," he told them. And with that he pulled aside a grass-woven cover and stood aside to reveal an array of foods prepared for voyaging. Alongside was a large stash of the weapons Ko'i had been fashioning over the years.

Pueo spoke. "We have been preparing and setting these foods aside. You will travel far, and you must catch fish and birds when you can and save this food for hard times."

Ko'i spoke next. "These tools and weapons are yours. Go to Oahu and bargain for more food, ropes, and other supplies. Find a crew of men and women who can sail and who are able to live on short rations. Keep the weapons of your choice to protect yourselves."

Next, the group, carrying food, tools and weapons, walked to the canoe shed where Haunani and her mother were waiting. A pile of woven lauhala sails and olona rope had been placed next to the big double canoe, and logs had been set at right angles in order to slide the great canoe into the water.

The young warriors who had accompanied Iaea to the battle were filtering back to Halawa in small groups. One group of twelve men, led by Kalani, came to Kolea and asked to crew the big canoe. "We expect to be hunted down by Mahi and would rather go with you," said Kalani.

Haunani, carrying one end of the huge rolled-up woven sail, came also saying that five of the young women of Halawa wanted to go as well. "I can paddle, prepare meals, do healing, and someone needs to know how to repair the lauhala sails," she said. "My friend Pualani wants to go as well."

And so a crew was formed, and as the people on Maui mourned the death of their king, the voyagers loaded supplies, gathered belongings, and said their farewells to family and friends. Each person brought two canoe paddles and all the kapa cloth fabrics they would wear. Villagers brought large bundles of ti leaves to serve as both spiritual and physical protection against the elements.

When the canoe was finally ready, Pueo chanted a message to the sea, and the villagers gathered to push the big craft into the sea. The men and women began to paddle the hulls forward, slowly at first, but then the rhythm of their training began to pay off and they were able to move the canoe out to sea.

"Who has the best voice to chant the paddlers?" Kolea asked. Everyone agreed that Pa'akiki was best, and the small man took up a position in the forward end of the platform connecting the two hulls and began to chant a cadence. At this, the paddlers came together as one, and the canoe surged forward.

"We will paddle until we reach Kalaupapa," Kolea said, "and then we shall try our big sail. We have much to learn about this craft."

"Kalani has appropriated the big steering paddle," Makanunui said. "With his strength he should be able to hold us in a blow."

The great canoe rounded the point of the Kalaupapa Peninsula just as darkness was falling. Kolea decided to beach the canoe away from the small village nearby and they proceeded down coast, where they found a protected steep beach. The crew beached the canoe and prepared a meal from the items their families had sent along. After they ate, they rigged some of the ropes Haunani had woven and stepped the masts that would hold the big crab claw sails.

CHAPTER 15

"WAKE UP," MAKANUNUI SAID.

Kolea rolled over in the sand where he had spent the night and cracked open an eye. "It's still dark, Makanunui," he groaned.

"Yes, but the wind is down and we can get the canoe off shore and catch a ride on the wind in an hour or so."

Kolea could not deny Makanunui's logic, but still he said, "All of us are sore from the battles and tired from our escape."

"Tired is better than dead," reminded Makanunui. "Let's get everyone up and get out of here before Mahi knows we are gone."

Soon the crew was up and fed, and they pushed the big canoe into waist-deep waters off Molokai. In the dim light, they pulled themselves into the canoe and paddled off the shore. Running without the chanting, they kept silent until they reached a point where the prevailing winds pointed them to Oahu. Then Kolea and Haunani pulled the big crab claw sail from its stowage, and together the crew fastened it to the mast and boom and raised it in place. Once the lines were tightened, the big sail filled and the canoe raced downwind toward Oahu.

Kalani had the big steering paddle down on one hull, and another of the crew kept a similar paddle in the water at the stern of the other hull. Up and down the swells the canoe raced, now slowing on the up side and speeding down the other. As the sun rose, the crew could see the mountains of Oahu and feel the surge of the big canoe as it powered its way toward windward Oahu.

The dark blue of the deep water in the channel began to turn turquoise as they approached the island, and Kolea asked, "How do we get past the reef?"

Kalani yelled from the stern, "I have been here with my grandfather. I know the way in."

So Kalani steered the canoe through a tight passage in the coral reefs and into Kaneohe Bay. The crew lowered their sail and paddled to the beach where some warriors, having seen the unfamiliar craft, were waiting with spears. Kolea told Pa'akiki to greet them with a peaceful chant, and the small man with the big voice stepped to the bows and began with a shouted greeting and a chant for a peaceful visit.

Haunani handed Kolea a lei of tiny moon-hued shells she had strung, and he carried a large twig with dried opelu fish strung on it and walked toward the leader of the warriors, laying the fish on a flat stone before him. "I have come in peace," he said. "I am Kolea, the son of Pueo and Koa Ko'i of Maui. My friends and I wish to look for additional crew for a voyage."

A voice coming from behind the line of warriors in front of him spoke. "Kanaka wai wai welcomes the son of Pueo and Koa Ko'i." The spears parted and an old scarred man strode through the line and embraced Kolea.

Kolea placed the lei around the chief's neck, leaned forward, and breathed an aloha into his face, mixing their breaths together. "E komo mai," the chief said. "Bring your crew, and we shall eat."

The warriors let down their spears and helped the crew ashore. Behind the line of coconut palms was a grassy area, and people were laying down banana leaves and placing bowls of poi and dried fish on the leaves.

Haunani and the women of the crew were led off to a similar but separate eating area, and all sat down to a meal. When their hunger had been satisfied, Kolea introduced Makanunui. "This is Makanunui, the son of Iaea of Halawa," he said to the chief. "He too has gifts for you." Makanunui came forward and unwrapped an axe he had made. It was a fine weapon, worthy as a gift.

A murmur went up from the assembled warriors when the axe was passed around. The chief stood and waved the axe around, striking imaginary opponents. "Auwe!" he shouted. "I have only seen one like this and it was used by Ko'i in a battle we once shared. Its balance is amazing. Who made this?"

Makanunui looked the chief in the eye and said, "I did. My kumu was Koa Ko'i."

"He taught you well," said the chief. "Did he teach you to fight as well?"

"He did," Makanunui replied. "But my best lessons were from my father."

"Ah yes," the chief said, smiling. "Let's see what you have learned." He beckoned to a warrior. "Get your ihe spear and stand over near that tree." The big man did so. "Makanunui will stand across from you. See if you can skewer him," said the chief with a laugh.

The warrior looked a little confused, but with some urging, he stepped forward and heaved the spear across the assembled diners at Makanunui's chest. With a movement hardly visible, Makanunui bent his upper body back, spun to the side and grabbed the spear as it passed within inches of his chest. He turned the spear around and he flung the spear back, embedding it in the tree not two feet from its origin.

"You are a branch from your father's tree," shouted the chief, waving the axe around his head. "I have seen him do that in battle just as I have seen the axe soldier wield these in two hands! You were taught well. Why don't you stay here and teach my warriors your skills?"

Kolea answered, "Chief, we are preparing for a long voyage. We have tools and weapons we wish to give you. We would take on additional crew who wish to go with us."

"Tomorrow," the chief said. "Get some sleep, and we will sit down and figure this out tomorrow."

The crew slept on and around the canoe that night. In the morning, they rubbed more oil on the hulls in anticipation of a long voyage. Haunani and the women of the crew spent time using a forked wooden stick to pull and tighten the fiber sennet that laced the gunwale strakes to the dugout hulls. Some of the strongest of the crew rerigged the mast stays and tightened all the lines.

Meanwhile, people from surrounding villages gathered carrying dried fish, freshly boiled taro roots, and bundles of sweet potatoes for the travelers. People from Kailua brought a huge net bag filled with coconuts along with big gourds filled with fresh water. The crew brought some of the tools and weapons crafted by Ko'i and Makanunui and gave them to the chief and his leading warriors.

By and by, a fine store of fresh and dried supplies began to show up. Bundles of firewood were passed on to the sand-floored firebox near the rear of one of the hulls. Kalani made sure a big bundle of sugar canes was loaded aboard as well. "I have to keep my good-looking body nourished," he said with a laugh. Haunani acquired additional bales of ti leaves for making rain capes and rolls of lauhala for repairing sails.

Many young people came to volunteer as crew. The prospect of an adventure drew them. Kolea, Makanunui, and Haunani talked to them. Kolea looked for people with broad shoulders and ample body fat as Pueo and Koi had instructed him: "Look for the people with the ability to paddle for long periods, and who can carry food reserves on their bodies." Pueo had also reminded him that slender people would not do well when the temperature dropped and the sea soaked them during storms.

Makanunui searched for people who knew how to rig and work the big sails. He also found a man who had the reputation of being able to catch fish when no one else was able. Haunani looked for women who were strong enough to work as crew and had the skills to repair woven sails and ropes. She also looked for women experienced and willing to have sex with crewmembers during the long voyage they anticipated and, in the tradition of the Polynesian people, to bear another generation in the event new land was found. Kalani came by and reminded her to get some good cooks, causing her to laugh.

At one point, Kanaka wai wai beckoned Kolea to the side of the gathering. "People who wish you ill have come from Maui in the night," he told the younger man. "It will not be long before Mahi will follow you here."

The old chief came closer and whispered, "I do not know all of the people who have joined your crew, but something smells bad to me. Watch yourself." Kolea, who had sensed this as well, nodded and drew a small sack from his bag. "Thank you," he said. "Please take this."

The chief opened the sack and cried out, "Auwe! Ala'ea salt from Molokai." He took a small pinch of the red salt and tasted it. "This is the best," he said. "I will keep this for myself and for my favorite wife." And with a great laugh he threw his arms around Kolea and wished him well.

The new crew spent the rest of the morning saying their farewells and gathering their belongings, and by midafternoon the canoe was loaded and afloat in Kaneohe Bay. Amidst chanting and waving from the shore, they paddled the heavy craft out into the bay.

Kolea stood on the bow platform and addressed the crew. "We are not following our kupuna's path to Kahiki," he said. "We are following the path of the kolea bird, which is beginning its yearly flight in the opposite direction."

"We are going to look for new lands," he said. "For those of you not willing, it is your chance to swim ashore. If you continue with us, you travel to the unknown place where the birds fly each year."

Kolea looked at the crew. "Are you with me?" A growl that became a shout followed as crewmembers banged their paddles on the gunwales and the voyage into the unknown began.

* * *

They paddled into the wind, getting clear of the reefs and islets before turning north along the Oahu shore. A strong, late afternoon on-shore wind kept them from hoisting the big sail and so they paddled long into the night, passing along the island shore.

As night fell, Kolea told some of the crew to get some sleep and kept the watch. The paddlers slowed, and Kolea kept the steersmen pointed north by watching the procession of star constellations moving from east to west, as he had been taught. The map Pueo had drummed into him during those long canoe trips when he was younger was giving him confidence now.

Halfway through the night, Makanunui relieved him and switched crew at the paddles. Kolea went to a place on the platform stretched between the hulls and fell asleep with Haunani spooned behind him.

The canoe proceeded along the shore, passing villages and seeing occasional fires set in cooking pits. As he slept, two of the new crewmembers, appearing to be asleep near him, soundlessly drew fire-hardened wooden spikes from their belongings and began slowly crawling toward Kolea and Haunani.

In her sleep, Haunani dreamed of the legendary mo'o, a large lizard believed to be in the deep valleys above Halawa on Molokai. She could almost feel the lizard crawling toward her and awoke to the small sounds approaching them along the deck. The stealth of the crawler warned her that whoever was crawling was up to no good. Quietly, she covered Kolea's mouth and squeezed his arm to awaken him. As she did so, one of the assassins lunged and struck her head with the blunt end of the spike. Haunani had moved quickly to the side, but the blow dazed her for a moment.

Like one of the black crabs he had seen, Kolea was on his feet and with a shout leapt across Haunani and knocked the first man down. The second man stabbed him behind the shoulder with a spike and as he did so he was swept off his feet by Haunani, who had recovered from the man's blow.

As the assassin went down, an enraged Kolea grabbed the man's head and jerked it sideways, breaking his neck. He grabbed the second man but stopped when he heard Makanunui say, "Wait! Don't kill him."

Haunani helped Kolea bind the man's arms and they questioned him. He told them that Mahi had sent word from Maui, saying that whoever killed Kolea would be given a chiefdom on Maui. He and his dead companion believed they could do the deed swim to shore and find a way to Maui for their reward.

At that, Makanunui ordered two crewmembers to take the bindings off and toss him overboard. "No," the remaining assassin cried. "If I do not die in the north shore surf, I will be shunned because some people know what we were going to do."

He looked at Kolea. "I am just a fisherman," he said. "I have gone along with my friend on a very stupid venture. If you let me live, I will be your slave. I will work alongside the others and go with you."

Kolea asked Makanunui and Haunani for their opinions and after they had agreed, he lifted the man and with his face close, he whispered, "What is your name?"

"I am Kepa," the would-be assassin answered.

"Well, Kepa, you will be a crewmember," Kolea said. "The first and only time you wrong me or any other crewmember, I will make shark bait of you."

With that, he untied Kepa's hands and ordered him to throw his dead compatriot overboard. When that was done, Kepa was assigned to paddle in the position closest to Kalani, where the big man could watch him.

As the sun rose, the big canoe passed beyond the island of Oahu and headed north under sail. With the North Pacific current and trade winds setting to the northwest, they pointed across it and followed the course of a small flight of golden plovers passing overhead. The canoe quartered the big swells coming from the west and set a rolling motion.

Haunani cleaned and dressed the wound in Kolea's shoulder. The crew trolled a lure off the stern and caught some ono for a fresh supper meal.

CHAPTER 16

THE FLIGHT OF the golden plover from its wintering grounds begins each spring when the birds, having fattened themselves over the winter, set out to fly far, far away, off to lands unknown—what we now know as western Alaska and Siberia. They joined birds traveling from as far away as lands now known as New Zealand and Australia.

On the second day at sea, Kolea watched his namesakes pass the canoe in strings of hundreds of birds, all heading at a ninety-degree angle from the path of the sun. Other smaller flocks of curlews and wandering tattlers were heading in the same direction. "These birds go north to breed. It means there must be islands that way," Makanunui said. "Maybe we will find our own." Kolea grunted an assent.

"How is your shoulder?" Makanunui asked.

"It's sore, but it bled well, and the oha wai nui salve that Haunani rubbed in the wound must be working, because it isn't swelling too much," Kolea said. The two men were trying to figure out how to split up the watches among the crew. The command of the canoe was Makanunui's, but Kolea was a king's son, and thus the two shared the duties. Kolea also had become a warrior leader and the crew respected him for his abilities, but all questions about the canoe ended up in Makanunui's lap.

After the island of Kauai disappeared off the stern, the travelers were on their own. Some of the crew were assigned fishing duties.

Fresh fish was eaten as often as possible so the dried supply could be saved. But food discipline was an issue. No one knew how long the voyage would take.

Haunani overheard the discussion and spoke up. "Give that duty to Pualani," she said. Kolea pondered that suggestion, but Makanunui began to laugh and said," Oh, nobody will argue with her. That's perfect."

Pualani was a large and powerful woman. She was not only capable of doing all of the traditional women's duties, but could swing the paddle under way as well or better than any man. Her reputation had been enhanced during one battle in Halawa village when an invader was gathering up her chickens. Pualani came out of hiding carrying a small log and killed an invading warrior with it. By having her take on the duty of giving out food, Kolea and Makanunui knew that transgressions from food discipline would be met with a cold silent stare. The culprit would give back the contraband without a whimper.

Even the imposing Kalani obeyed her and was soon on a rationed diet with all the others. Kalani had another reason for obeying Pualani. At night the two of them would go to the small privacy shelter between the canoe hulls and the sounds of their raucous coupling would cause smiles to break out among the crew.

With the exception of Kolea and Haunani, most of the men and women on the voyage shared sexual favors with one another. Many of those activities did not lead to pregnancy. A choice to have a child was a serious matter. Although the rearing of children was shared among villagers, a child had to know his genealogy.

At night, Makanunui directed that the canoe be steered toward Kio Pa'a, the polar star. All of the sky seemed to rotate around that point, and on clear nights the direction was easy to follow.

The familiar southern sky began to fade toward the horizon as the canoe traveled north. On cloudy nights the sails would often be furled and the crew rested, but when they were under partly cloudy skies they continued on. Kolea and Makanunui remembered the rising and setting points that were taught to them by Ho'okelo during their boyhood canoe lessons.

As long as some sky could be seen on either eastern or western horizons, the rising and setting points gave the crew good general directions, and the canoe made progress. But after four days and logging a good hundred miles each day, things changed.

Kolea shook Makanunui awake. "Look at the sky." A dark storm front was gathering from the northwest. Crewmembers pulled the boom and sail to the mast and lashed it. The storm seas crossed a current going toward the northwest and caused an immediate rise in the steepness of the seas. All supplies were moved into the hulls and battened down, and the canoe began to blow eastward.

Kalani kept the bow pointed downwind and the canoe surfed the waves, but doing so was a trial. Kepa, the former assassin, came to Kolea and quietly made a suggestion that seemed to be a good one. Kolea and Makanunui carried a fishing net back to the stern and Kepa rigged a harness for it. They tied some small mats to the netting, pitched some spare items into the net for ballast, and deployed it off the stern as a sea anchor. The canoe came around to a steadier course and Kalani had an easier time, using the steering paddle to make corrections.

For the following two days, the canoe traveled eastward. Paddlers worked hard to keep the canoe steady as it rose on the backs of the seas. None among them knew how far they had traveled, but when the storm dissipated in the next night, they read the sky and found themselves farther north but some unknown distance to the east. So the paddlers pointed north, the sail was unfurled, and the canoe crossed the westward current and sailed into the convergence zone that we know as the North Pacific Gyre.

For two days, the winds were favorable, and the canoe made its way north. But then the winds and currents began to die down and paddlers were called on to work in shifts as the canoe traveled on. During the day, Kolea and Makanunui each took a turn at the paddles while the other commanded the canoe.

At one point, it became hot and still and their water supplies were being called upon in greater amounts. During the storm, Pualani had collected rainwater in big bowls and refilled the drinking gourds. But they all realized that water would soon become an issue.

For a week, they paddled north. The bird migration had passed. Kolea and Makanunui navigated across the sun's daily path and they used the polar star at night. They were no longer catching large fish as they traveled far from any shore, but Kepa, who turned out to be the best fisherman, discovered that schools of fish no bigger than a man's forefinger were sheltering under the shadow of the canoe. He rigged a small mesh scoop net, lowered it through the space between a canoe hull and the platform, and came up with hundreds of small fish that could be eaten fresh.

Kepa had his head down under the platform, manipulating his net, when he gave a great shout, rose up, banging his head on the underside of a log, and yelled, "Kohola," just as a huge humpback whale surfaced in front of the canoe and blew. All Kepa had seen was a sleek black back with barnacles stuck on going right beneath the canoe, yet he had known.

The crew looked around and found that they were in the midst of a traveling pod of humpback whales headed for their feeding grounds in the North Pacific. Kolea said, "Follow them for as long as we can. They are going somewhere and it will likely be along a shore just like they enjoy at home." They followed until the last whale disappeared and they could no longer see its spout.

Along the way they encountered floating logs and wood debris gathered in the water, so the steering oar got a lot of use as the paddlers pushed the canoe through the center of the Gyre and beyond to the north. Some firewood was gathered from limbs sticking up from the floating trees. Water and food rationing had begun to cause some grumbling among the crew, and the constant paddling was wearing them down. An occasional dispute led to minor scuffles. Pualani was called upon to referee and to separate the combatants.

Eventually, Kolea called a halt and ordered a day's rest. The canoe floated still in the water and crewmembers swam and relaxed for a while, easing tensions. Someone spotted some exhausted curlews resting on floating logs, and some well-aimed sling stones brought them as fresh meat to the crew. They pulled the embers from their stone container and lit a fire in the sand box, then roasted the birds on a stick over the fire.

The crew sat together and shared some of the cooked birds. Kolea told them that they were committed to go on and find the place where the birds and whales had gone. "Going back is no longer an option," he said. "I have faith in what Pueo told me. We will continue."

"Look!" Pa'akiki shouted while pointing up. The smoke from the firebox was going up about ten feet and then drifting off on the first wind they had seen in a week of paddling. The women who were eating had seen the breeze as well and had beaten the men to the mast and were unfurling the crab claw sail.

Out went the boom, and the sail slowly filled and the canoe began to move. A cheer went up as Kalani grabbed the steering paddle and brought the canoe before the wind. Men and women got to their stations and began to paddle. With the light winds filling the sail and the paddlers rapidly working, the canoe headed north. The wind became steadier, paddlers were given a good rest, and Pualani rationed out some of the last of their water.

Makanunui and Kolea consulted at the bow of the canoe. "We need a rain," Kolea said.

"I think we'd better go to it because it's not finding us," Makanunui said. Then he dropped a small weight on the end of a piece of sennet and noticed that the current that had been going to the west before they entered the calm area was beginning to move them to the east. In the distance, he could see clouds close to the water, and so they sailed a course across the wind and with the current and headed for the cloudy area.

The next day, crewmembers stayed still under lauhala mats to try to conserve their energy, but some of them had begun to show signs of dehydration. One tried to walk off the stern of the canoe and had to be restrained. Night fell and the canoe moved eastward in the darkness. The stars began to disappear, and in the early morning a light rain began to fall.

Pualani spent the morning at the base of the big sail gathering water in bowls and handing the bowls to Haunani and others to refill the water gourds. Crewmembers spread their lauhala mats above their paddling stations and ran fresh water onto their bodies for their first cleansing in weeks.

When the water had filled all containers and the crew had drunk their fill, they ran before the wind and headed north.

CHAPTER 17

THE TEMPERATURE DROPPED and the rains came as the canoe moved to the northeast. Crewmembers wrapped themselves in kapa cloth and finely woven lauhala matting. Haunani and the women of the crew broke out the baled ti leaves and made rain capes. And the canoe continued on.

After more than twenty days at sea, both food supplies and morale were in short supply. An occasional tired migratory bird would make its final landing on the canoe and provide a snack for the crew, but otherwise the supplies were nearly gone and people were weakening on short rations. The currents carried them north and spilled them into an eastward flow.

Kepa had finally caught some fish, pulling two large salmon from his lures trailing the stern. They were preparing to eat them when Kolea heard an odd sound, something he had never heard before. Much to his surprise, more than a dozen orcas were approaching the canoe from the stern. The whales swam in a diagonal formation, with one leader coming farther out of the water each time they came to the surface to breathe.

As Kolea watched, when the leading female approached the canoe, she came out of the water, perhaps to get a look at the strange contraption. When she did, Kolea grabbed one of the big salmon and tossed it to the whale. She grabbed it in mid-toss and swallowed it in one gulp and led the pack onward to the east.

Kalani looked shocked, shaking his head at the action. "The whale was looking for something to eat," Kolea said. "If not the fish, then you are the most appetizing thing on here."

The crew believed that the orca would know where there would be more fish, and so they followed the whales and were pleased to find themselves in a school of king salmon. The ravenous crew ate their fill and started a cooking fire to preserve some for the future. Just then the wind began to increase from the west so they doused the fire, rigged backstays to hold the mast more securely, and sailed in the direction the whales had gone.

Curious, Makanunui asked Kolea why they were heading east. "Listen," he said.

Above the sound of the wind in the rigging, Makanunui could hear them. "Birds," Kolea said. Ahead was a flock of hundreds of terns. They were diving on schools of the small fish that had attracted the salmon and the orcas. There were also gulls with black legs feeding, and at one point the seas picked up, the small fish left the surface, and the gulls began to fly off to the east.

"Look at those strange clouds," Makanunui said. On the eastern horizon they could see a triangular white shape.

"Those are not clouds," Kolea said. "It is a white mountain, like our Mauna Kea." The wind drove them onward, and more snow-covered mountains began to appear in a line stretching as far north and south as the eye could see. As they got closer they saw a great forest below the snow line and rocky cliffs behind an inlet in the shore.

Kolea turned the canoe over to Makanunui's command. They pulled down the big sail and moved on under the bare mast and paddlers. Makanunui ordered all crewmembers into their paddling stations and had all cargo battened down as great gusts blew them toward the shore.

Pa'akiki shinnied up the mast and told them they were headed for a sand spit with trees on it, but there was an apparent entrance on the right end. The sound of large breakers could be heard as they approached, and Makanunui gave directions to the paddlers and steering oars to get them to the bay entrance.

As they approached, another sound of rushing water could be heard, and a great flood tide picked them up and shoved them toward the entrance. The canoe was now under the command of the tide. Great eddies and whirlpools twisted them this way and that until the canoe struck a rock in the entrance channel, smashing one hull. The canoe tipped sideways, dumping most of the crew into the water, and then righted itself as a great wave swept the broken canoe into Lituya Bay.

Haunani and seven crewmembers survived by hanging onto crossbeams. Pa'akiki experienced the ride of his life hanging onto the mast. Kolea was unconscious and lay tangled in some of the lashings. One hull was destroyed but it was still afloat, and they were drifting in calm waters toward the head of the bay. But Makanunui, Kalani, Pualani, and the remainder of the crew were gone.

As soon as they could, Haunani and the surviving crewmembers rigged a small sail and, paddling the wounded boat, they limped toward an island in the middle of the bay. They passed floating masses of ice and seals and landed the damaged boat at a small beach on the rocky island.

CHAPTER 18

WHEN NEXT KOLEA opened his eyes, he found the strangest face he had ever seen bent over looking at him. Much to his astonishment, the woman had a plate of whalebone inserted in her lower lip, and she wore a flat cone-shaped woven hat and a short skirt woven from bark.

He had an enormous headache and he was surprised to find bruises on his body where there should have been none. The woman was feeding him a broth. Haunani was seated next to him, he discovered, and other crewmembers were seated by a fire nearby, eating some fresh-cooked meat and a concoction of berries and seal oil.

"We have no idea what she is saying, but she is being very kind to us," Haunani said when she knew he was awake. "She appears to be the only one on this island."

Kolea sat up, but the woman gently pushed him down, shook her head and forced him to drink the herbal soup she offered him. After he drank the unfamiliar concoction, he fell back asleep and awoke again hours later. That time he stayed awake, and upon looking around he saw that he was inside a shelter backed up against a cliff. The dwelling was made of driftwood logs propped up against the rock wall and the joints were stuffed with mud and moss. An open fire against the rock wall warmed the interior and a door flap made of some kind of animal skin closed out the rain and wind. And it was cold.

Haunani, he saw, was crouched by the fire trying to communicate with their hostess. "What happened?" Kolea asked her.

She got up and came to sit by him. "As best as I can tell, there are great tides here that wash in and out twice each day," she said. "We came in at the wrong time. Only ten of us are here on this island."

"Where are the rest?" he asked.

Haunani began to cry and took a while before she could speak. "They were swept into the sea," she replied. "I don't know if any others survived."

"What about the canoe?"

"One hull made it. The other was smashed beyond repair and we lost most of the cargo. At least the good hull had weapons and tools. Everything else was lost."

Shaking his head at the news of his friends and crew, Kolea then gestured at the strange woman. Haunani spoke. "I believe this woman is an outcast. She calls herself Ka'atoowa'a. She was left here by her people, who believe she is some kind of witch, and she lives here alone. We call her Ka'a. You have been asleep for two days."

He considered this and nodded. "Is there food?" he asked, for he realized he was very hungry.

"That's the good news," Haunani replied. "There are fish here of all kinds. Our crew is fishing from the shore and the woman is showing them how to smoke and prepare the fish. But I believe the fish will not be here for long and we must lay in some supplies."

They heard a shout and Kolea staggered to his feet. Haunani gave him her shoulder to help him out and they stepped outside.

"Smoke! There on the beach!" Pa'akiki shouted. Across from the island along the shore a couple of miles away they saw a fire burning and thought they could make out some tiny figures near it. The crew on the island had fashioned an alder driftwood log into a makeshift ama outrigger and had taken four of the iakos and were lashing and bracing them to the dugout to make an outrigger canoe.

Much as he wanted to go investigate, Kolea's legs felt weak. "Those are sea legs," Haunani said, nodding. "It will take you a day to get them back."

Kolea sat by the canoe and used a forked stick to tighten the lashings while Haunani made a smaller sail from the remains of the wreckage. Ka'a was helping Pa'akiki with the work on the lashings and Kolea detected a smile on Haunani's face. "I believe she has chosen Pa'akiki," she said.

"He doesn't seem taken aback by her strange appearance," Kolea said.

"Nor would you after a month without me," she said with a laugh.

The following day, the canoe cobbled together was ready. They loaded some smoked fish and some berries they had gathered and waited for the tide to ebb. Ka'a came with them, carrying a pointed paddle with strange pictures carved on it.

They launched and paddled to where they had seen the fire burning. As they approached, Kolea was excited to see Makanunui, who ran to the shore along with two other men and a woman, members of their crew. They were clothed in makeshift capes made from pounded bark twined together. He embraced Kolea and wept openly.

"Come, we need help," he said. They walked up behind the fire pit the survivors had made and found several more of their crew. Pualani and Kepa were there with the others, curled up and moaning.

But one more of their crew was still missing, Kolea saw. "Kalani?" he asked.

"Swept away."

Pa'akiki used a rubbing stick to light another fire, and they fed the crew the smoked fish and berries with seal oil they had brought with them to the shore. "I don't know what happened. Some of them are very sick," Makanunui said.

Ka'a looked at Pualani, writhing with discomfort, and walked back to the beach. She brought back a fresh clamshell and pointed at it with a questioning look. Pualani nodded, and Ka'a tossed the shell aside and shook her head. She looked at Haunani and said something while gesturing. "They are poison," Haunani guessed. "When did they eat them?"

"Just now," Pualani said. As the others watched, Ka'a reached into a skin pouch she carried and brought out some herbs. She gave them to the victims and gestured for them to swallow them with lots of salt water. They did so and almost immediately began to vomit and continued to spew until at long last they threw up clear fluid.

Looking satisfied, Ka'a nodded and beckoned them back to the canoe. She pointed at great tracks in the shore mud that led west and gestured with her fingers bent into claws and her teeth chopping. From that Kolea guessed that there was a creature there that they did not want to encounter, at least not yet.

The flood tide was nearly finished and so the reunited crew, in the overloaded canoe, had an uneventful paddle back to the island. Haunani directed the erection of a tent made from sail remnants and salvaged matting, and a fire was started next to a rock face where the crew could gather for warmth.

A short canoe expedition around the island with their fishing lures trailing brought back a big halibut that they filleted using Ka'a's jade knife and pegged it onto driftwood next to the fire. Someone had also dug up the corm of a skunk cabbage plant that reminded them of taro, and they baked it and ate it. After getting a meal down, the people who had eaten the bad clam meat were improving but still looked weak.

CHAPTER 19

THE TRAVELERS FROM the Hawai'ian islands had difficulty pronouncing the guttural and click sounds of Ka'a's language, but through gestures and patience they were able to communicate what was important. Haunani turned out to have a knack for languages and was soon speaking simple phrases in Tlingit, as the woman's tongue was known, and the two women became close.

On a calm sunny day, the crew paddled the makeshift outrigger canoe to the inland head of the bay where it divided north and south. On both ends of the T-shaped bay stood walls of ice. Kolea and his crew were astounded. The ice loomed two to three hundred feet above the water. They were looking at the faces of two great glaciers that wound down the valleys from snowfields high on the mountains.

Once in a while, with a sound like thunder, the ice would come loose and fall into the water with a huge splash, and a wave would roar out from the ice but dissipate in the deep water. Small icebergs were all around them, Kolea saw, and some would roll over, causing them to steer the canoe wide around the bergs.

Hundreds of seals lay about on the floating ice, and some could be seen giving birth to their pups. With hand gestures, Ka'a instructed the island travelers in seal hunting, showing them how to use an inflated seal stomach float she had brought. The float was tied to a piece of line connected to a small lance. Makanunui, the most accurate spear thrower, became the harpooner in the bow of the canoe, and they soon had a load of seals to take back to the island.

When the seals had been skinned, the women began scraping the hides while the men butchered the meat and strung it up to dry. As best she could, Ka'a explained to Haunani that when winter came, the ice and snow would come as well and they would die if good shelter, food, and clothing were not available.

As they prepared for the coming change of season, the crew soon realized that many of the ways they had brought with them were no longer workable. Making shelter for what would be a winter like they had never experienced would require men and women to work together and move the heavy pieces. And if clothing were to be available, men would be doing much of the sewing as well. The kapus against eating together were maintained, but many of the others were dismissed by Makanunui and Kolea.

They dug and split long slender spruce roots and coiled them, storing them in water for use as cordage and basket making. And they took instruction from Ka'a on how to preserve the huge cache of food they had gathered.

Next, on a foggy day, they discovered the clawed creatures that Ka'a had told them about. Ka'a had described the great bears to them, but the islanders were used to their own myths and legends, which included unseen giant pigs and lizards, and so they put the warnings in the same part of their minds. There was no denying the evidence of tracks on the beaches of the bay shores they explored, but they could not imagine the likes of a bear simply from its tracks. Still, they carried their ihe spears with them on the shore expeditions.

On one sunny day they had canoed ashore hunting for edible roots and greens along the fringes of a grassy meadow when they spotted two brown cubs tussling in the edge of the deep grass. Ka'a signaled to the travelers to back away, but the cubs were so attractive that they stayed just to watch the cubs play.

All of a sudden, a huge sow brown bear stood up from the grass nearby and bellowed. The cubs were off running into the grass in an instant, and the bear dropped down onto all fours and began running toward the intruders.

Everyone began to run. Pualani, the slowest, was run down by the bear and was given a swipe across the buttocks by the sharp claws.

Kolea shouted and the others stopped. They quickly organized and grouped closely together. The formation began to advance on the bear, their spears poised, and they began to chant a prayer of protection. The sow bear stood over Pualani, bared her teeth, and huffed in threat, but beat a slow retreat when the shuffling, chanting warriors came toward her.

They helped Pualani to the canoe, and Haunani and Ka'a cleaned the cuts she had suffered. Back at their settlement Ka'a used an unguent on the sliced buttocks, and they closed the wounds with a small bone needle and some animal gut. Ka'a explained as much as she could that the male bears were much bigger, but that a female with cubs was more dangerous. Makanunui realized that the door covering on Ka'a's shelter was the hide of a large bear, and he wondered who had killed it. On the following day they found out.

It all began with the sighting of an unfamiliar canoe. On a slack ebb tide the canoe had entered the dangerous entrance. The boat was unlike any they had seen. The single hull with ten paddlers was flared on the sides and had high wave-breaking ends. It was decorated with carvings and painted in red and black. A figurehead in the totemic shape of a growling wolf sat atop the wave-breaker bow.

Ka'a told Haunani to get the travelers out of sight, so they armed themselves and moved into the verge of the forest. The paddlers were disciplined and all swung paddles similar to that used by Ka'a. When the canoe came to the beach, Ka'a greeted the apparent leader. They embraced. The leader, having seen the outrigger canoe and other evidence of occupation, kept his warriors at their paddling stations while he conversed with Ka'a.

She called to Haunani, who emerged from the forest, spear in hand. When she got to the couple, Haunani stuck the back end of her spear into the ground. Ka'a said—for by then she and the Hawai'ian travelers had become acquainted with the language of the other—"This is my brother."

She gave Haunani his name, which consisted of many syllables, and then she added, "we call him T'ooch'. If my father knew of his visit he would be angry. Bring the others."

Haunani waved and the other travelers came from the forest. When they reached the beach, they all planted their spears. When T'ooch' saw the gesture, he ordered his paddlers to disembark.

That was when Kolea spotted Kalani. He was trussed up in the rear of the big canoe and was badly bruised. One of Kolea's men saw him as well and shouted and grabbed for his spear, but Kolea barked a command. The man quickly put the spear back into the ground and stepped back.

T'ooch' held up a hand to restrain his men and spoke to Ka'a. "I found this one on the open ocean beach and made him my slave. It wasn't easy. He is as strong as three of us,"

At this, Kolea had to decide what to do to get back Kalani, for his tradition was not based on trading. But he recognized what was happening and explained it to Makanunui, who headed back to the shelter with another of the travelers. When he returned they were carrying some of the new tools and axes Ko'i had sent along.

"Tell him I would like to buy his slave," Kolea said, and he handed one of the war axes to the leader. A Tlingit warrior was called forward to examine the axe. He looked it over carefully and swung it about before handing it to another man who also examined it and passed it around.

The leader asked to see the other weapons and tools. He spoke to his sister. "He wants all of these and your spears in exchange for this valuable slave," Ka'a said.

Kolea, recognizing the negotiation for what it was, tried to look perturbed, scratched his head, and answered, "Tell him the slave was the laziest of my men and ate too much, but I am willing to trade two axes for his worthless body."

T'ooch' smiled and countered, "Two axes, one adze, and your spear." Kolea pondered the offer and then nodded. He pulled his spear from the ground, handed it to T'ooch' and told Makanunui to give the axes and adze to the leader. Then he gripped hands with T'ooch' and Kalani's release was ordered.

The two crews sat down for a meal, with Haunani translating. T'ooch' filled them in on Ka'a's exile. When ice had pushed forward, damming the stream miles above his father's summer village, the salmon the people had depended upon for years for sustenance no longer returned in great numbers. Making matters even worse, the water building up behind the ice dam broke through from time to time and flooded the village site.

"My father had to have someone to blame, and so he chose Ka'a," her brother said. "She is the wisest and most capable of our storytellers and is an excellent healer, both for the body and the spirit. But some of the ignorant people look askance at those skills. And so she was exiled in order to set nature back in balance."

Kolea asked the obvious question. "Did the fish return?"

"No, and the floods came back. So the village is being moved, which I had suggested, but my father is a stubborn man and it took another flood to get him to order it. I have been counseling him to bring my sister back, but he is not yet ready. So each year I bring her supplies and have a short visit. My father knows I am doing so but chooses to ignore it."

After an evening where each group examined the boats and weapons of the other, the Tlingit warriors slept on the beach and left on the outgoing tide in order to transit the entrance at the slack.

It was fall and the weather was turning cold, the likes of which the travelers had never felt. Ka'a's brother had left two large sea lion hides, one of which served as a door for the larger shelter. With two helpers, Makanunui had started on a second canoe hull, roughing out a big spruce log they had cut on the island. He had spent days watching woodpeckers banging away on the trees and had chosen one the birds had ignored, knowing that it was one that was ready to be used.

As the weeks went by, they knew they had to have as secure a shelter as possible, for some of the women knew that they were pregnant. They found out one early morning when they were not the only ones sneaking out to vomit on the beach. Haunani had been carrying her child since before the trip started, and with the alder leaves falling, she judged she would no doubt have her child by the end of the year. Pa'akiki shared lodgings with Ka'a, and in her womb she carried a half-Tlingit, half-Hawai'ian baby. In addition, Pualani was pregnant with Kalani's baby and two other women, who had paired up with crewmembers, were showing pregnancy as well.

Ka'a guided the crew to a small stream loaded with small oily fish. Kepa brought a scoop net and harvested baskets of the fish and strung them on twigs to dry. Ka'a explained that they would serve as lanterns when needed. They also gathered huge piles of firewood and splinters of sapwood to make starting the fires easier. Haunani began sewing boots from the second sea lion hide, taking a pattern from a worn-out pair of Ka'a's boots. They also fashioned clothing like they had never needed back home, in the form of parkas and pants from the seal hides they had scraped and cured. An aging brown bear had swum to the island and been killed by Kalani and Kolea, and that hide had been made into a sleeping rug for Pualani. The first snowfall was a gentle one that piled wet snow on their dwellings. The travelers were delighted and frolicked in it, tossing snowballs and sliding down a steep slope on a discarded lauhala mat.

But the novelty soon wore off and the big coastal storms and surf forced them to haul their canoe into the forest and to secure all of the supplies, for they realized harsher times were coming. Kolea saw the warriors getting bored with it all and so to keep them alert and energized he organized a trail around the small island.

Each day the warriors ran the trail and did exercises with their spears. Makanunui and others worked under a makeshift canoe shelter, scraping and cleaning the old hull and carving a mate for it. Kolea began each day lifting stones and soon was joined by the others. But as the days grew short they slept longer and spent a great deal of time in the shelters talking story.

CHAPTER 20

WINTER HAD PASSED. The daylight had returned, and the salmonberries were leafing out. The sounds of babies mingled with the sounds of canoe carving. Haunani's child was born within the great bear rug placed out on the small sand beach, and Kolea named him Nene'au kai after the black-legged gulls that guided them to their island and that nested on the cliffs nearby. Pualani's girl was stillborn, much to her sorrow, and Ka'a believed the unborn child had been poisoned by the clam sickness. But Pualani recovered and soon was again carrying a child within her womb.

Two other children had been born into the tiny but growing community. Ka'a and Pa'akiki had a daughter they named La'akea, after the northern lights that had streaked across the sky during the night of her birth. Those lights, too, were amazing to the travelers.

The canoe hulls were being lashed together, and women and men both were plaiting new sails from reeds they had found near a small lake on one of their shore expeditions. The island seemed a fine redoubt from bears but when fishing or seaweed gathering, people always traveled with the long spears ready.

Makanunui had found some fine abrasive stone, and crews were rubbing the hulls to smooth the wood. He also concocted a purple paint using the fish oil and blueberries and after ten coats and rubbing, the canoe was finished and spectacular. Kolea chanted what he could remember from Pueo's launching chant, and they named the canoe K'eet, the Tlingit name for the orca. One of the crew suggested carving a killer whale for the wave breaker bow, like the Tlingit vessel, but Ka'a told them the orca would consider a realistic carving a ridicule and after having seen the orcas up close, they decided not to do it.

They sailed K'eet back and forth in the bay, getting used to the new boat, and when on the shore, they constructed a platform of cedar and began to fit the boat out for cruising. That little island was too small to build a growing community, and they discussed where they could find a better place. The discussion ended when the canoe bearing Ka'a's brother came back to Lituya Bay.

When T'ooch' came ashore, his crew looked exhausted. He was limping and his leg was bloodied. Others were also wounded, Kolea saw. "What happened?" Ka'a asked.

"People from the lower islands came to attack us. Some of our people were taken as slaves, and the survivors have scattered."

"What about our father and mother?" Ka'a asked in alarm.

"They were taken as captives," her brother answered.

Haunani and Ka'a helped T'ooch' to the shelter and cleaned and treated his leg wounds. Others of the Tlingit wounded were treated as well. Ka'a went to Kolea and told him that when her brother was recovered, she would go with him to find their parents. The travelers were welcome to stay on the island.

Kolea thought for a moment and then replied, "In our home, where we are from, there is a time to grow food, a time to honor our leaders with taxes, and a time for war. You are now part of our family and your kindness saved us from our own ignorance about this new land. If there is a fight ahead, we will fight with you."

And so while the Tlingit warriors healed their wounds, the Hawai'ians prepared their weapons and made new spears to replace the broken ones. They gathered stones for the slings and packed the ropes and matting they had been working on all winter. Kalani brought out two new steering paddles he had been carving, and soon the canoe was loaded with their belongings.

A strong shelter was in place to hold the babies and their mothers. When all was ready and the tide was right, they bade farewell to their island and with their canoe followed the Tlingits down toward the entrance. The sails were furled, and they paddled through the channel they had missed on their way in. The end of the ebb was meeting swells from the west, and they had to break through the waves and set crew to bailing, but they were soon outside the breakers and in a fair wind headed south.

The Tlingit canoe had no sail, and so the Hawai'ians paddled behind them, navigating the swells as they moved south. They passed one glacier that came right to the ocean shore and calved ice in the water. But most of the ice was held along the beach by the onshore wind and did not create a hazard for the two boats.

Both canoes took a diagonal tack away from the shore to stay clear of coastal bays with their tidal currents and to avoid rocks. In the afternoon the lead canoe turned into a channel through some rocks and entered a small bay, which afforded protection from the sea and wind. Pa'akiki and Kepa had caught some big salmon on their trolled lures, and the Tlingits erected some planks next to a driftwood log. They started a fire next to it and split the salmon in half, pegging the fish to the planks.

A bear was attracted by the smell but was sent running by a barrage of stones and shouting. The two crews enjoyed a salmon dinner along with dried deer meat and strawberries that were growing in scattered clumps along the beach edge. Guards were posted to watch for intruders and bears, and the crews slept above the high tide line.

In the early morning, they got under way to take advantage of calm waters and very little wind. The lead canoe passed some big rocky islets and turned left into a broad reach that opened eastward toward some larger islands and narrow channels. They crossed to the southwest and entered a mile-wide channel with mountains rising on both sides.

On a signal from the Tlingits, they paddled along the shore until they came to a point that stuck out, obscuring the southern portion of the inlet. After beaching the canoe, they waited while a scout made his way inside the tree line. When he returned, he shook his head. There was no enemy. They boarded their canoes and paddled to the beach in front of the village. They knew what they would find by the smell wafting from there.

CHAPTER 21

THE SURVIVORS OF the village attack came out from the forest when they saw T'ooch'. They were wary of the Hawai'ians and stayed clear until they saw Pa'akiki helping Ka'a and her child climb down from the canoe. There were a thousand questions from both sides. The villagers told their stories and Haunani and Ka'a translated as much as they could.

Several Salish canoes filled with warriors had attacked the village early in the morning and the fight had been uneven, the survivors said. T'ooch' and his crew were some of the only warriors to escape. The rest were either taken captive or, in the event they were wounded, put to death on the spot. Women and children had run to hiding places, and the attackers had set fire to the houses. There were seven warriors who had been on a hunting trip when the attack took place, and upon their return they searched for survivors and gathered who remained and they were now burning the corpses. Some of the women were constructing a shelter from the remnants of the destroyed longhouse, the center of the village, and there was a temporary tent made of matting in which the children were huddled.

The only canoe left to the Tlingits was that of T'ooch'. The others had been commandeered by the Salish to carry the captives. Kolea's canoe was assigned six of the Tlingit warriors and the remainder joined T'ooch' in his boat.

After provisioning the Tlingit canoe, they paddled back the way they had come into the inlet and turned east into the narrow passage in pursuit of the Salish. A strong tidal current pushed them through the channels at high speed with the paddlers working to keep the canoes stable and away from eddies and whirlpools alongside the channel. Their route took them past the face of the largest glacier they had seen, and they steered around many icebergs.

After a full day of paddling, the two boats landed at a tidal river where a small summer village was situated. The foreland was half ice and half forest, and there were meadows and openings where people hunted deer and gathered berries.

The people of this place were related to T'ooch' and Ka'a and welcomed them. Children had been gathering strawberries along the beach two days before and had spotted the Salish canoes and sounded an alarm. The tide and a brisk wind had held the boats off long enough for the villagers to carry their camp and food supplies into the woods, and the Salish, finding the camp abandoned, had gone across the sound toward the big village to the east.

In the morning Kolea suggested to T'ooch' that he board the double-hulled canoe and let them sail across the sound, towing the Tlingit canoe with a steersman left in it. They gave it a try, and with the wind coming down off the great glaciers at their stern quarter, the K'eet did what Makanunui had designed her to do and flew across the great sound at several times the speed they could paddle.

T'ooch' knew the waters and they avoided reefs and rocks, and the man steering the Tlingit canoe was able to keep it steady, although it occasionally yawed. T'ooch' navigated them along a shore on the north side, and they furled the sail and reloaded the Tlingit into their canoe. When they came to a point shielding them from the big village, they beached the canoes.

T'ooch' asked Kolea and Haunani to accompany him, and they walked around the point on a bear trail just inside the forest. They climbed some rocks and saw that half of the Salish fleet had left and the others were busy hunting for survivors and pillaging. No one, they noted, was guarding the canoes.

Kolea suggested that they set a trap for the remaining Salish warriors and outlined his plan. T'ooch' agreed, and they went back and gathered their own warriors. Some women were left with the babies, but Haunani and Pualani came with them.

They followed the path to the edge of the village. Once they got below the high beach line, they were not visible from the village. Kolea instructed the women to get in the smallest of the slender canoes and pretend to steal it. He then deployed the Tlingit warriors on the flank and had his warriors crawl below the beach slope and line up on the ground near the canoes, their spears ready.

At his wave, Haunani and Pualani ran to the smallest of the canoes, pushed it into the water, and climbed in. A shout came from the village and several warriors came running. As they rose over the embankment, the Hawai'ians attacked as one and skewered the Salish. One man wove his way through, but when he tried to climb in the boat, Pualani hit him on the side of his head with a paddle, and he dropped into the water and drowned. When a second wave of warriors came to engage the Hawai'ians, they were attacked by Tlingit warriors from the flank, and in the surprise attack those Salish were either killed or badly wounded.

The ruckus had drawn the remainder of the Salish, and they stood back, their weapons poised. Their leader came through the ranks and called out in Tlingit. "Who is this?"

"I am T'ooch'. You have stolen my father and mother and many of my people," was the reply.

"I will give you a choice," the Salish leader said. "Fight me with no weapons, and if I win, we leave. If you win, you do as you wish."

T'ooch' put down his weapons and advanced into the space between the warriors. The Salish leader did the same. They traded blows for a while with no one getting the advantage. Then T'ooch' rushed in and grabbed the Salish leader around the waist, lifted him, and threw him to the ground. They rolled, and once the Salish leader was on top, he drew a hidden copper dagger from his clothing and tried to stab T'ooch'.

In a movement so fast he was nearly unseen, Makanunui jumped to the middle, snapped his garrote around the Salish leader's neck and strangled him while Kolea and the others surrounded the remaining Salish warriors, who had dropped their weapons.

T'ooch' questioned one of the villagers, and she identified those who had killed noncombatants. Those warriors were taken to the beach and killed. The remainder were taken as slaves.

CHAPTER 22

WHEN THE SURVIVING Salish warriors had been tied up, Kolea sent Pa'akiki climbing up a bare spruce snag for a look. He reported that the Salish canoes and two Tlingit canoes carrying the captives were headed south across the sound toward an inlet. He also reported that the canoes of the Tlingits who had been gathering food at their last night's stop were headed toward them from the west.

When all of the canoes had arrived, T'ooch' and the chief of the village consulted with Kolea to make a plan. "They do not like the open passage to the east," the local chief said. "In a heavy wind their narrow canoes take on too much water. And they are carrying trussed-up slaves in our canoes but from the looks of it, they have little experience handling the bigger canoes."

With that, T'ooch' drew a map in the dirt and showed them where the Salish would likely follow a bay to the south and then portage across a narrow place at high tide, thus avoiding the big waters to the east. "It will take some time to drag the canoes across the portage," he said.

They decided to take the long route through the big water and intercept the Salish in the narrow sheltered bay east of the portage. Haunani, as the only interpreter, went with them, leaving her child with the other women. When the warriors were loading into their canoes, Pualani, carrying a stout short spear, began to climb on the K'eet. The Tlingits assigned to the Hawai'ian canoe asked why the woman was coming along. Kalani let out a whoop of laughter and told them that if they valued their limbs they wouldn't question her. Haunani translated, and with a shrug from the Tlingit the canoes were off.

One Tlingit warrior acted as pilot, and they paddled east until Pa'akiki could no longer spot the Salish canoes from his climbs on the mast. "They are behind the islands in that bay," the pilot said. The sail was unfurled and the K'eet leapt forward, leaving the other canoes behind. At the intersection with the big channel, running north and south, they picked up a wind from the north, passed outside a dangerous reef and ran at an even faster speed to the south.

At evening they turned west into the entrance of the channel they anticipated the Salish would come out from and paddled into a small sheltered bay to await the following canoes. In a narrow deep inlet they tied the canoe to trees on both sides so they would not go aground when the tide changed. There they waited.

Feeding down to the shore was a creek and nearby was a pool situated above the tide line with vapors rising from its surface. Some of the Hawai'ians, having seen such a thing back home, swam ashore and found a hot spring feeding the creek. They moved upstream and located warm water that would not scald them and soaked away their aches and pains for a couple of hours. When the Tlingit canoes arrived, they posted sentries on some high rocks to watch for the Salish, ate a meal, and then slept on their canoes. Then Kolea and the Tlingit leaders plotted their next day's battle.

During summer, the nights were short in the region of the Tlingit homeland, and after only four hours, the Salish canoes were seen coming east. The K'eet was unleashed, paddlers with their weapons at their stations, and they waited. At a signal from a sentry, they unfurled the sail, picked up a favorable breeze, and moved out of the bay, banging their paddles on the gunwales and chanting. Makanunui stood on the bow of one hull and Kolea on the other.

The warriors on the Salish lead canoe saw an apparition like none they had seen before. The K'eet, piloted by two large warriors with tattooed faces, was on them before they could get their weapons up. Kalani steered the K'eet to the rear, drove the port hull over the low stern, and the weight of the big double canoe pushed the Salish canoe into the water and dumped her crew. The Hawai'ians jumped to the mast and furled it while others paddled the boat around to face the second and third Salish canoes.

As they did, the two Tlingit canoes drove out from hiding and cut the Salish off from their prisoner canoes. They boarded the captive canoes and made short work of the paddlers. After freeing the captives, they joined the battle.

As the K'eet passed alongside one Salish canoe, a Salish bowman got off an arrow, which hit Pualani in her bicep. When he saw this, Kalani, in a rage, swapped his huge steering paddle with Kepa's and jumped into the Salish canoe, where he began pummeling the paddlers, starting with the steersman and working his way forward. One warrior stabbed Kalani in the chest, and Kalani yanked the copper knife out, threw it behind him, and snapped the warrior's wrist before throwing him into the sound. Someone on the K'eet lassoed the bow piece of the canoe. They pulled it alongside and subdued the remaining warriors.

But another Salish canoe had come up the other side, its warriors fighting their way onto the K'eet. A Salish warrior threw a spear at Makanunui. He dodged it, caught the spear, and sent it back at twice the speed into the chest of the man who threw it. Kolea was wielding two clubs as Ko'i had taught him and soon, the fight was over.

T'ooch' found the Salish chief. He had been wounded and could no longer fight. "We came to revenge a raid made by your people," the chief said.

"We have not raided you," T'ooch said.

"Not in many years. But we do not forget," the chief replied.

"You stole my father and mother, and I cannot let you go," T'ooch' said.

"I accept my fate," the chief said. "I would prefer to die rather than to be a slave." And with that, he rose up and T'ooch' plunged a jade dagger into his heart.

"Take their weapons and put the Salish back in their canoes," T'ooch' instructed. He wrapped the chief's body in a ceremonial blanket, carried it to the Salish canoe, and told the paddlers, "Take this chief home and bury him with his clan. I have no need for more slaves, and we are now even. Do not come back."

With that, he shoved the first canoe off and the second followed. Then the Tlingit canoes and the K'eet paddled ashore, where they buried their own dead and tended to the wounded. Pualani's bicep had been pierced by the arrow, and Haunani had cut off the point and drawn the shaft back out. She packed the puncture wound with healing herbs and then tended to Kalani, putting healing medications on the stab wound and sewing it closed.

The next day they left on an early morning tide and paddled back the way they had come. They left the sail furled and took lessons from the Tlingit pilot on the use of tidal currents in the area. The K'eet stayed together with the Tlingit canoes, and by the next evening they were back at the village where they had left their children and women. There were happy reunions of people who believed they might never see one another again, and wailing and tears for those killed in the battle.

But there was one serious negative issue as well. When the old chief saw his daughter Ka'a, he yelled, "What is she doing here?" T'ooch' explained she had brought the Hawai'ians to the village and that she was no longer an exile. "She has disobeyed me and must not live," the chief said.

At that, Ka'a pulled her baby out from her woven robe and hugged him, indicating that the chief had a grandchild. Her mother stepped in front, glared at the chief, and reached for the child. That was the end of the argument.

Later, Kolea asked Haunani what had transpired. She smiled and told him, "In their society, the clans are derived from the mothers' line. She has more power than her husband in matters such as this."

He was about to reply with a rash remark about male dominance when he saw a look on her face and decided against it. A feast was prepared and gifts were given to the Hawai'ians. Grieving widows of warriors killed in the battles were given to unattached Hawai'ian crewmembers, and they came willingly, as the future of a widow among the Tlingits was not a good one.

Haunani and Ka'a advised Kolea that the Hawai'ians needed to prepare for winter. Ka'a said she was now part of their family and would go with Pa'akiki wherever he went. They knew that if they stayed they would stress the resources of their hosts who nonetheless were begging them to stay, so they packed the K'eet and departed on the morning flood tide, heading back to the east and south.

The Tlingit chief told them they were welcome to winter in the area with the hot spring, and so they sailed there and got to work preparing shelters and catching and drying fish.

While scouting the beaches in the inlet they came upon a sorry sight. Next to a damaged Salish canoe beached by the falling tide sat a forlorn boy of fifteen or sixteen. He had clung to the canoe and was washed ashore with it after the battle. Ka'a spoke to him in Salish and found he was raised on the Haida Gwaii, captured by the Salish in a raid and brought along as a slave.

Kolea took him back to the encampment and warmed him in the warm stream and fed him. The boy willingly pitched in on the building and food gathering. Because they could not pronounce his Haida name, they named him Keiki Loa'a: the found child.

CHAPTER 23

SEVEN YEARS HAD PASSED since the day the Hawai'ians had spotted the tops of the Alaskan mountains. The present winter had come with a vengeance. The cold rain was followed by a hard freeze that turned the shore into an ice-covered slope. Nene had survived the cold winters but some of the other children had not. Pualani had borne another baby, alive and healthy, and had given him the name Kili after the fine rain that had fallen on her when she had gone to the beach for his birth. Kili was now a good size and was known as "little bear" among the Tlingit women.

Because of their battle on behalf of the Tlingits and the rescue of the captives, they lived under the protection of the Tlingit people. Ka'a's clan and its relatives made frequent visits during summers, and the K'eet had explored much of the territory around the northern sections of the waters. But there was a melancholy hanging about the Hawai'ian community, so far from their homes and for so long.

Makanunui had salvaged the broken Salish canoe, designed and built an outrigger and a sail rig for it, and the narrow canoe was used for hunting and fishing expeditions as well as short trips to visit nearby villages. Makanunui was busy finishing work on a larger double-hulled canoe to take the place of the K'eet, which was not fit for another long voyage. Kolea had become the de facto chief of the village. Daily fighting exercises were performed, and the men of the village took instruction from him and from Makanunui on weapons. Haunani did the same for the women.

On yet another cold day Kolea worked alongside Makanunui in their canoe shed. The shed was covered with snow, and a fire in the rear kept some heat in the place. They lashed the wash-strakes onto the new hulls and caulked them with spruce pitch mixed with fibers Haunani had pounded from bark. "I saw a pueo owl hunting over the big meadow near the portage yesterday, and it seemed to tell me something. I believe we should prepare to move south when this winter is over," Kolea said.

Makanunui paused and said, "Your mind is in the same place as mine. I often think of my father and mother and wonder if it is time to return."

Kolea pondered that thought. "I suspect that Mahi has a long memory and that the myth of the king's death is now a legend believed by all," he said.

Makanunui smiled. "Not if Pueo and my father have anything to do with it." They laughed and continued pulling tight the lashings.

Haunani came into the canoe shelter. "What am I going to do withNene and Kili?" she cried.

"What now?" Kolea asked.

"They took some worn mats and were sliding on the ice. They talked Ka'a's daughter into joining them, and she slid right into the icy water. I heard them yelling and we pulled her out and put her in the hot pool to warm her."

"Is she all right?" Kolea asked.

"She'll be fine, but those two boys are driving us all *pupule!*"

"I'll talk to them," Kolea said.

That evening, the two boys started formal schooling. Kolea began by teaching them simple story chants as Pueo had done for him. As the winter weeks passed, he continued with the creation chants. The boys enjoyed the attention but when they slid back into mischief mode, Kolea brought them up short, telling them that this was how they would become men and warriors, not by plaguing the women. And like successful students everywhere, as they plied their minds to their schooling, their attention span began to lengthen, and the care given them by their chief gave them a comfort in learning that they had not experienced before. As spring approached, the boys were taken out on a canoe at night and began learning the chants about the stars.

The Tlingit women had taught Haunani and Pualani how to make tanned deer hides and sealskins into winter clothing. Haunani, in turn, taught the Tlingit women and girl children plaiting and ropemaking, and they began to make large sails, weather covers for the paddlers, and coils of rope and sennet. Early runs of large king salmon were caught, smoked, and dried for future use, and shoots of spring fireweed and dock were boiled and eaten to give the bodies of the Hawai'ians strength to chase away the winter doldrums. They had also found many edible unfamiliar varieties of seaweed and had dried them and bundled them for supplies.

Pa'akiki worried that Ka'a might not want to accompany him on a return voyage across the ocean, but she was adamant, as were three of the other Tlingit wives. "I am content," she said. "There is no place for me in my father's heart. My people have had many expeditions to the south and I never enjoyed staying behind." However, two of the wives chose to take their children and join their families in the Tlingit village. In the Hawai'ian tradition of hanai, most of the children were given to Tlingit families and moved to their home village.

After tens of thousands of years of occupying the islands of the Pacific, the concept of a larger land that seemed to have no end—known later as continents—was foreign to the Hawai'ians. But the Tlingit people spoke of their tribal relatives who lived well inland, and in their travels, the Hawai'ians had become comfortable with the geography of the larger land. Experienced Tlingit navigators who had been on extended trading voyages had given them instructions on the nature of the coast.

Makanunui and Kolea agreed that they would go south through the islands and follow the coast until they were under the nighttime path of Hokule'a, the navigation star, and then would proceed west across the ocean, following their star home.

The new craft that had been constructed had two masts and sails and after a launching ceremony, it was named Kio Pa'a for the polar star, which had been their most reliable guide during the seven years they had been in the north. They took it on some short cruises and learned its idiosyncrasies. Just as the past efforts of Makanunui had been, this craft handled well, and it worked even better on many points of the wind. The new double canoe was given multiple coats of fish oil until they reflected the spring sun.

At the time of the year when the daylight became equal to the dark of night, they paddled the big canoe out into the inlet and caught a fair wind from the north. Under only one sail, the canoe surged forward, and with that they left their northern home behind.

CHAPTER 24

MEANWHILE, AT THE TIME the Kio Pa'a was sailing from their northern home, the marriage of Mahi to the daughter of the ruling chief of the island of Hawai'i had stopped the constant raiding and warfare between the two islands. Mahi's wife was endowed with more mana and a superior family history to that of Mahi, and he was required to be subservient in her presence. This grated on him and caused him to take out his frustrations on his subjects.

To touch the king or even his shadow was a capital offense. Under King Nanoa there had been almost no infractions. But people now knew they would suffer the most serious penalty for any violation of the kapu. One elderly man who had inadvertently walked across Mahi's shadow had been beaten to death by the squad of ruffians and lua fighters that accompanied King Mahi wherever he went.

The king's share of crops and fish payable as taxes grew each year until it burdened the farmers, causing much discontent. But the fear of retribution kept people in line and they worked harder than ever to meet increasingly unreasonable demands.

Without worries from the warriors of the Big Island, Mahi sent out expeditions to Molokai and Oahu. His warriors had landed on the leeward side of Molokai and gained a foothold at Pukoo. But warriors from the windward side had attacked from the mountains and driven the Maui contingent out onto the plain at Kawela, where much blood was shed before Mahi pulled his warriors out and returned across the channel to Lahaina. Many warriors returned to Maui, having heard the tales from Iaea's people that Mahi had actually been responsible for his own father's death.

Pueo Luahine had spread the same story through the dancers and priests of her persuasion. Mahi's spies told him as much and he began plotting to invade Halawa and the rest of Molokai through the windward side of the island. He offered a substantial reward to anyone killing Pueo, Ko'i, or Iaea.

Mahi had commissioned a war heiau to be built at Honokohau at the far end of West Maui. The big stone structure had been laid out by the priests so it faced the island of Molokai across the channel. Mahi believed it would increase his mana to the point that he could sweep through Molokai and on to take Oahu and Kauai.

Many tons of rock had been carried to it in preparation for the building. Mahi was presiding over a blessing and sacrifice cere-mony in which a slave was killed and buried under each corner of the structure. He demanded the opportunity to kill the slaves himself, and had bludgeoned all four to death and had them placed in the corner holes and covered with stones as the structure began.

When his bloody task was finished, Mahi bathed himself in the bay's salt water and sent his thugs into the countryside to find suit-able girls for his entertainment. Two of the three warriors returned with girls, but somehow they lost track of the third.

The third warrior found himself in a taro farmer's place up in one of the valleys. When he demanded to take the daughter to the king for his entertainment, the girl's mother refused. The warrior grabbed the girl's arm just as the taro farmer was rounding the corner of his house to see what the commotion was about. He found the warrior and the farmer's wife pulling on the girl's arms from both sides.

The farmer was a wide man: very heavy and very strong. While the warrior was occupied in the struggle, the farmer grabbed the warrior's spear and broke it over a rock. Then he got his substantial arms around the warrior's waist, drove him into the taro patch, and stuffed the man's head into the mud until he stopped breathing.

The girl's mother had brought back the true tale of King Nanoa's death from her sister, who was a novice dancer in Waiehu, and they were certain that they would have to leave Maui if Mahi remained the king. The three packed their belongings, left their farm, and went to their canoe landing. They loaded up their things and headed for Molokai.

At Halawa, the farmer related what he had seen about the building of the heiau and what they had all heard about Mahi preparing for a major invasion. Iaea thanked the man and had him taken to one of the vacant taro growing areas and furnished the family with food and a temporary crew to get the taro patches prepared and planted.

A council of war was held and the chiefs of Molokai made plans to deal with a coming war.

CHAPTER 25

TWO THOUSAND MILES to the north, the Kio Pa'a had been traveling behind some large islands, but Kolea had followed the directions they had been given by the Tlingit navigators, and finally they came to an open sea and headed south into it. Great swells began to pick them up and drop them and the wind picked up speed from the west. As they reached the tops of the swells, they could see the mountains behind them. But soon they were scudding out of sight of land and under a cloudy sky with no sun. Kolea assumed the wind was coming in from the open ocean on the right, so he kept the canoe on a south heading.

The crossing of the big entrance had been rough. The children had been secured inside the deck shelter and during the turbulence they had turned the color of the gray sky and vomited until they had no more strength and had fallen asleep, exhausted. Makanunui had furled the sail to the mast but the two masts still acted as sails, and the wind and seas pushed them east. The men and women of the crew paddled the canoe to try to keep it pointed southwest and they had a fear of blowing onto a lee shore, or some unknown rocks or shoals.

"Listen!" shouted Kalani from his steering seat at the stern.

Kolea heard the sound of surf off to their left. He gave a signal and the crew paddled for their lives, and the big canoe narrowly missed blowing onto a surface shoal. The wind and incoming tides carried them into an area of sand islands, and the exhausted paddlers worked their way into the lee of a long narrow island covered with a dense forest. They beached the canoe, secured it to some trees, and collapsed on the beach.

Pa'akiki started a fire, and the children were warmed and fed while Kolea and Makanunui explored the shore. The Haida boy who had joined them, Loa'a, was now a man, and he accompanied them. "This is Tsimshian territory," he said. "We shouldn't stay here long." They followed the bear trail that looked heavily traveled just inside the beach line and saw signs that people had been on the island, but not in recent times.

Kolea held up a hand and they stopped. Five deer were browsing the beach grass ahead of them and Kolea told the warriors to stay still while he crept through the trees facing into the wind. When he was close enough, he reared back and threw his spear into the side of one of the deer.

Loa'a quickly skinned and dressed the deer and they walked back on the beach to the canoe. Kepa fastened the deer onto an alder stick and they roasted it over the fire. After sharing a good meal, they decided to rest for a day and made camp above the tideline. The children and women slept in the shelter on the canoe while men slept by the fire, keeping sentries on each side of the camp.

Kolea awoke to a gentle shaking. Pa'akiki was kneeling next to him, giving a sign of silence. He whispered, "There is someone in the forest watching us."

"How many?"

"I only see one and he is quite still." Kolea nodded and sent him back to his post.

Kolea lay still for a time and then yawned, arose, and headed into the forest as if to relieve himself. In almost complete silence he moved around behind the place Pa'akiki had indicated and saw a small figure crouched behind a fallen log.

Abruptly, he moved behind the figure and seized him in a tight grip. In a flash, Pa'akiki was in front of the figure with a spear at his throat. When they removed the elaborate wooden hat the person was wearing, a very old man stared back at them.

The old man spoke a language they did not understand. His knees were shaking, and he looked weak. Kolea and Pa'akiki brought him back to the camp and asked Loa'a if he could understand what the old man was saying. "He is a Lekwiltok man," was the reply. "He was left on this island to die and has been eating berries to stay alive."

Kolea had the old man fed and then they sat with him, and with Loa'a translating, they listened to his story.

"I am a shaman," the elderly man began. "My village is many days' paddle to the south. I was brought along in a fleet of war canoes making raids here and across this water." He gestured to the west.

Loa'a added, "They were raiding in the islands of the Haida Gwaii, where I am from."

The old man continued, "We had a sea battle with the Haida and were winning when some strange sea currents and a wind from the west scattered our canoes and caused the Haida to get the upper hand. Our chief, an incompetent war leader, had to have someone to blame, so when we were blown here by the weather, he put me ashore and left me."

"Ask him if he knows these waters and directions," Kolea said.

"I am a Lekwiltok shaman," the old man repeated. "Of course I do. The fool who leads our war party will be lucky if he can find his own penis, much less find his way home."

When the last was translated, Makanunui rocked back and barked with laughter. "Oh yes! I have known kahunas just like this one," he said. "Ask him if he will go with us."

When asked, the Haida man shook his head, turned to Kolea, and replied. "He said he must consult a bird first and that he knows that Kolea will understand," said Loa'a.

After he had eaten, the shaman led them to his camp and retrieved his paraphernalia. From a large bentwood box, he retrieved a strange mask and a rattle, put the mask on, and began to chant and dance.

"What is he doing?" Kolea asked.

Loa'a replied, "It is a blessing for us."

Makanunui asked about the elaborate mask. "It is a bird, a loon, and the bird can transform itself into a human."

Kolea had a start when he heard that, thinking about Pueo and the many times she had guided him in the past. When the shaman was finished with his dance, he stowed his mask and rattle back in their box, picked it up, and headed to the canoe, where he hoisted it onto the boat and began to inspect the hulls while muttering to himself.

Haunani and the other women were weaving repairs for their sails, which had been battered during their voyage south, and a crew of men was using forked sticks to tighten the lashings on the iakos and the wash-strakes. Others dug edible roots that the Tlingit wives knew of and baskets of blueberries and bog cranberries. Kepa had caught some small humpbacked salmon they had found spawning in a small creek and had split them and pegged them to driftwood next to their campfire.

Kolea had sentries posted on both sides of the encampment and one on the beach across the narrow island. With the exception of a surprised black bear that had been drawn to the smell of cooking fish and was chased off, they had an uneventful few days while they made repairs, rested, and gathered food for the next journey.

CHAPTER 26

THE CREW PADDLED from behind their sand island and left on the low slack tide, picking their way through the shoals and rocks and into open water. The shaman directed them due west. They set sail and found a morning wind coming down off the mountains behind them, so they headed for the Haida Gwaii. The Kio Pa'a drove into the incoming swells and the crew battened down the supplies, secured the children in the shelter again, and fastened their woven spray capes to the gunwales for the ride.

Within the first hour Makanunui could tell that the canoe was sailing into shallow waters. Tidal rips carried them one way and then swept them back the other way. They had learned to deal with such things during the years in the north, and so the canoe carefully wove its way toward the northern tip of the Haida Gwaii.

Heavy rain and the cloudy sky kept them from seeing the sun, but the shaman seemed to know where they were headed and they followed his prompts. The feeling of the sea seemed to change, and Makanunui lay down in the bottom of one hull, felt the motion of the waves, and determined that the land was southwest of them.

As they turned southwest, the swells from the sea diminished and they came in sight of the northeast cape of the Haida Gwaii. Loa'a came forward and told them that his village was far to the south in a string of islands that projected into the sea, so they turned south, furled their sail, and paddled just off the coast.

On the shore, a Haida man had spotted their strange craft and reported to his village. A call went out to the surrounding villages and the clan warriors reported to their canoes and gathered at the landing. The matriarch of the village was a cautious and experienced trader, and what she envisioned was a capture and an addition to her already substantial wealth. She instructed her brother, the village chief, to follow carefully along the shore and, when the time was right, to bring her goods and slaves.

The Haida had few equals in the design and construction of their canoes. The massive yellow cedar trees gave them single log hulls capable of carrying fifty or more people and their skill at sea battles was well known as they traveled up and down the coast and passages, raiding and carrying slaves back. Three canoes with more than a hundred well-armed paddlers slipped out of the bay and rounded the cape in pursuit of the Kio Pa'a.

The leading canoe kept the top of the mast of the Kio Pa'a in view and was able to follow unseen as the boats paddled alongside the beaches on the east side of the large island. When the Kio Pa'a slowed and turned to a beach for the evening, the Haida leader did the same, unloaded his warriors, and waited. A scout was sent through the forest and was told to return when the strangers were bedded down for the night. Then the Haida warriors ate a meal and prepared for battle.

In three hours the scout returned and gave his report. "These are people I do not recognize," he said. "They are tall and wide and one is gigantic. They have among them some Tlingit people and a Lekwiltok shaman. There are a few children as well. They have set out sentries."

The leader pondered the situation, and called for his own shaman. "Do you have your bear robe and mask?" When the shaman nodded, he instructed him to do two things: prepare the warriors so they would not be seen or injured during a battle, and to bring the robe and mask with him. In silence, the shaman danced a protective dance with his rattles muted, and the troop headed into the forest.

Before they reached the sentry, the leader instructed two thirds of his troop to go back into the forest and wait. When they heard the shouting and commotion, they were to surround and take whoever was left in the camp. He told them not to harm the people, because to do so would diminish their value as slaves or hostages.

As the warriors crept silently into the forest, the shaman, clothed in his bear robe, his mask in place, moved with great stealth toward the Hawai'ian sentry. At a distance of twenty feet, the Haida shaman rose up and began clacking the movable jaws on his mask and making a horrible sound.

The hair on the sentry's head stood straight up. He dropped his spear and screamed when the apparition appeared before him. The camp was instantly awake and, in the darkness people grabbed their weapons and ran toward the shouting. When the Hawai'ians had left the camp, Haidas came out of the forest and surrounded the women and children in such numbers that it was no contest. But a battle was joined in the forest and after slowly backing away, the Haidas disappeared into the trees. Kolea turned and ran back to the camp to find the women and children gone.

A voice called from the forest. Loa'a translated, "He says for you to put down your arms and we will not harm your people."

"Are these your clan?" Kolea asked Loa'a.

"These are raiders," he replied. "They are not of my clan. They take from us and steal our women and children for slaves."

Kolea grabbed Makanunui and Loa'a and slipped into the forest with them just as the Haida came out into the open. The leader gestured for the men to get in the canoe and to follow the Haida boats that now held the women and children.

In the moonlight, with twenty armed Haida on board, the Kio Pa'a was paddled along the beach behind the war canoes. As they started, Haunani heard bird calls from the forest and knew that Kolea was following them.

The Lekwiltok shaman had heard the calls as well. The Kio Pa'a was short-handed, and the Haida warriors assigned to the canoe were not used to the paddles or the rhythms needed in the low hulls and so the procession moved slowly. Kolea and his companions were able to travel on the edge of the forest and keep them in view. Haunani had warned the women and children not to make a fuss.

As the little fleet turned west at the north cape, the swells met them, but shortly they turned into a bay and were in calm waters. At the head of the bay stood a village, and on a high point overlooking the bay was a fortress made of logs. Sharpened stakes stood out from the base, and lookout stations were located above. The people from the Kio Pa'a were herded into the fortress and separated.

The matriarch and her brother, guarded by a retinue of armed warriors, entered the fort and spoke to the assemblage, asking, "Who is your leader?"

To the surprise of the Hawai'ians, the Lekwiltok shaman pointed to Haunani and said, "This one is. She and her crew captured me and are holding me hostage." Ka'a stepped behind Haunani and whispered, "These people are led by women. Play their game."

So Haunani stepped forward. "Bring your interpreter and come with me," said the matriarch's brother. As she turned to go, the matriarch looked down and saw spots of blood on the sand. She walked to the women and saw blood on the inside of Pualani's leg. "Put this one in the women's enclosure, but keep an eye on her," she said. And with that she instructed for lookouts to be posted on the upper stations and with Haunani and Ka'a, she left the fortress.

Pualani was warned that if she tried to escape, one of the others would be killed. She was taken to a small enclosure where menstruating women were cloistered. The women were a little wary of the Hawai'ian woman who was half again as large as any of them, but one came to her with an offer of food and Pualani accepted and thanked her.

Finding that they could talk, the curious women asked her where she had come from. Pualani explained that they were from the sea and had been living in the north for several years, but were trying to make their way home. The Haida women spoke among themselves and agreed that Pualani, because of her strength and beauty, was destined for marriage among the Haida rather than slavery.

Haunani had been led to a huge longhouse, where she told the matriarch the same story Pualani had related. She was questioned about the purpose of their visit to the Haida Gwaii. Haunani told the woman that they were from far across the western ocean and were headed home.

"How far are these islands you speak of?" asked the matriarch.

"It took us twenty days to come here," Haunani replied. "But the return will be longer because we must go south to catch favorable winds."

At that point the matriarch understood that these were not prisoners for ransom. They would become her property, and from the looks of them they would have great value. Haunani was returned to the fortress, where the food supplies had been brought from the canoe.

While the prisoners were having a meal, Kolea, Makanunui, and Loa'a found a good hiding place from which they could observe the village. They noticed that the Kio Pa'a had been tied to a mooring anchored in the bay to prevent the Hawai'ians from launching it.

Makanunui climbed a big spruce tree and could see into the fortress when the gates were opened. He saw the captives bound together with cordage and climbed back down to report what he had seen. "I don't believe they will be bound up for long. Haunani has taught them all how to make and handle rope and they will free themselves," he said.

Kolea puzzled for a while and said, "Remember what Ko'i taught us? If we are captured, it is better to make our escape as soon as we can. It gets more difficult as time passes. Where are their canoes?"

Makanunui told him they were on a sand beach just west of the village and that there did not appear to be guards posted there. "I recall an escape from my childhood, and there is no reason it can't work here," Kolea said. They gathered armloads of dried lower branches from the shore pine trees and hid themselves in the forest until the following evening. Kolea instructed them on how the plan would work.

As night began to fall Kolea climbed the spruce tree and bird-whistled into the fortress. He heard a reply from Kalani and climbed back down. The three walked quietly to a point where they could observe the canoes, and Makanunui used a rubbing stick to ignite some small pitch-laden sticks.

While Makanunui started the fires, Kolea and Loa'a gathered the paddles from all the canoes but one and placed them in the last canoe. They stacked the armloads of sticks in the empty canoes, sprinkled some seal oil they found in one boat around the fires, and split up. Loa'a and Makanunui paddled the big canoe away from the beach and waited while the fires caught hold.

A sentry on the forest tower sounded the alarm and mass confusion ensued. Villagers carrying baskets for water were running to the burning canoes. Kolea came out of the forest carrying a Haida paddle, and he faced the guard at the fortress gate. When the guard lunged at him with his spear, Kolea crouched as he had seen Ko'i do, spun around, and swung the paddle, breaking the guard's ankle. . Then he opened the gate and released the prisoners, who had freed themselves from their bindings.

Quickly and quietly, he led them through the village in the darkness. Pualani, who had broken down the door to her enclosure, joined them. He instructed the Hawai'ians to swim to Kio Pa'a and get her ready to depart. The others met Makanunui and Loa'a at the edge of the village, climbed aboard the Haida canoe and, after dragging aboard the Lekwiltok shaman who had arrived late, paddled to Kio Pa'a.

As the Haida canoe made its way to the Kio Pa'a, several arrows were launched from the shore when a few Haida warriors had discovered their escape. Loa'a yelled at them to duck below the gunwales and paddle with one hand. They made their way slowly to the Kio Pa'a, where the swimmers had loosened the boat from the mooring and distributed paddles to all the stations. The crew, with the experience of more than seven years of paddling, moved into position and paddled off, towing the Haida canoe.

CHAPTER 27

THE KIO PA'A MOVED off into the night with the crew stroking the paddles in unison, and they disappeared from the chaos of the burning boats. Haunani grabbed the Lekwiltok shaman and asked him why he lied to the Haida about being kidnapped. "I had no value to them," he said. "Those Haida buy and sell people based on value. If I had told them I was an exile, my brains would now be decorating a big stone outside the village."

Loa'a overheard and said, "The old man is right. This clan only cares about their belongings, and that includes slaves."

"I have no people now. If you take me with you, I will do whatever I can to help," the shaman said.

"Then get up in the bows and help look for a route to the south. Keep us off the rocks and shoals," Kolea said.

Makanunui headed them out into deeper water and away from the shore and riptides, and the Kio Pa'a picked up a wind and moved along the eastern shore of the Haida Gwaii. They paused near their previous camp, paddled the Haida canoe ashore, and recovered weapons, food, and the shaman's box of paraphernalia they had left when they were captured. After paddling back to the Kio Pa'a, they tied the war canoe behind them and headed south.

Kolea decided that going ashore for the night was risky, so the crew drifted in the current and rested during the short period of darkness, and in the morning they moved south toward Loa'a's village. The wind had died, and a fog developed, which caused them to slow their progress. "We are near my home," Loa'a said.

The shaman asked for silence and they listened to the sounds of tidal water moving and the sound of birds. After a loon called its mournful sound, the shaman pointed them in a direction and they paddled blind into the fog. A flock of small gulls was gathered on the still water dipping for tiny fish, and they moved silently past the birds.

"There is a narrow opening to our bay and we should be close," Loa'a said, his voice oddly loud in the gloom. Makanunui could catch glimpses of the shore now and then, and he began to feel the flood current carrying them toward an opening in the shoreline.

Kolea silenced the crew and ordered them to simply paddle to control the movement and be prepared to back-paddle hard if rocks appeared. In almost total silence, the canoes drifted into the bay in front of Loa'a's village. The tops of the clan's totem poles were visible above the low fog, and the crew paddled to the shore just around a point out of sight of the village.

Village children spotted them and ran to the village. Kolea told the crew to keep the canoes away from the beach and he went ashore with Loa'a. By now, the alarm had been sounded and the two of them were met by the vanguard of ten warriors.

Kolea and Loa'a put their hands out in front to indicate they had come in peace, and Loa'a spoke to the men. He gave his Haida name and stated, "I was captured by Salish raiders six years ago and rescued by these sea-people."

At that, a woman wove her way through the ranks and looked into his eyes. Tearful, she embraced him. "This is my son," she said. "He has returned from the dead."

Women gathered around Kolea and began to touch him, curious about his size, a foot taller than the other men, and he became uncomfortable.

In the broken Haida language he had picked up from Loa'a, Kolea asked, "Who is the leader of this village?"

An older man stepped forward and said, "I am."

Kolea said, "I have brought a gift and would like to bring it ashore."

"Do so," said the man. "You are welcome here."

At that, Kolea walked back around the point and shouted to Makanunui, "Bring Kio Pa'a to the village landing." When they had done so, Kolea had the Haida war canoe untied and brought around to the beach. "Please take this canoe as our thanks," he said.

The Haida warriors gathered around and Loa'a told them of their capture and escape. They hauled the canoe ashore and began hacking the clan totem off the bow and scraping the painted symbols from the hull. Villagers crowded around the Kio Pa'a and marveled at the double hull. The elderly chief pulled Kolea aside and using Loa'a as an interpreter, he said, "It is a brave thing you have done. But the former owners of this canoe are very bad people. They will get other clan canoes and will be after you. It will be dangerous for you and for us if you remain here." Kolea nodded.

The villagers brought dried salmon in bundles and berries mixed with seal oil in bentwood boxes. They fed the crew and the chief gave Kolea a copper dagger, and to Makanunui, he gave a jade finishing adze.

With full bellies and a stock of food, the crew of the Kio Pa'a left the village on the ebb tide, turned around the outer point and continued their voyage to the south.

As the Kio Pa'a followed the shore, the island narrowed into a peninsula and then became a string of islands. The Lekwiltok shaman advised them to paddle through a passage to the open sea, where they would avoid dangerous rips and treacherous sea conditions. They furled the sail and Kalani steered the canoe to the west and they entered the passage. About halfway through the narrows, Ka'a had a bad feeling about the move and shared it with Haunani.

As Haunani moved forward to talk to Kolea, however, it was already too late. The Lekwiltok shaman had sent them into a trap. Three Haida war canoes paddled into the narrow passage and blocked their way. Other Haida warriors came out of the forest on the north side of the passage, and the war leader who had captured them earlier was among them. Kolea yelled at Kalani, "Come forward and steer from the bow." Then he ordered the paddlers to turn and paddle astern. Haunani and Pualani ran to the deck shelter and covered the children with woven mats, ordered them to stay put, and grabbed their spears.

Kolea tried to keep his cool, but the subterfuge by the shaman pushed him over into a fearsome anger. The old man was trying to crawl under the mats with the children when Kolea found him, grasped him by the feet, and flung him into the water. One of the Haida canoes had surged ahead, and a bowman was shooting arrows into his crew. Shouting curses in Hawai'ian, Kolea reached into the cooking box, grasped a fist-sized stone and hurled it at the bowman, striking him in the chest and knocking him backward into the paddlers.

The second canoe had slowed to pick the shaman out of the water, but the third was trying to get abeam of the Kio Pa'a in order to give their bowmen a chance to send a fusillade of arrows and spears into the crew. Makanunui had jumped up on the platform and was shouting, "Paddle for your life!"

A Haida warrior from the third canoe hurled a spear at him as a cheer came up from the Haida paddlers. The cheer was short-lived. Makanunui appeared to have no bones in his back as he bent backward, captured the spear in an iron grip and with a great shout hurled it back at the Haida, striking one of the paddlers in the throat.

As the battle approached the east entrance to the narrows, the earth began to shake. Kolea could see trees on the shore begin to wave back and forth as the earth shook. The waters in the narrows started running west, and thousands of wavelets appeared all around the boats. A loud roaring sound began to come from the sea. "Kahinali'i!" Makanunui yelled.

The crewmembers from Halawa had more than enough experience with tsunamis that had visited their valley back home, and they paddled harder. Just as the water had run westward it stopped, and the crew paddled hard for the east end of the narrows. The Haida warriors also had extensive experience with tsunamis, and they put ashore and ran for high ground. They were too late.

"Hang on to something!" Kolea yelled as he grabbed the spare steering paddle and dug in next to Kalani. The roaring sound grew and a great wave washed down the narrows just as the Kio Pa'a was reaching the opening.

And then, as if time had slowed down, Kolea looked over his shoulder and saw the wall of water coming. There were men and a canoe inside the wall and he realized that they might be joining them.

But then an amazing thing took place. Kio Pa'a, just as its prede-cessors had done for millennia, rose up and surfed the wave. Kolea and Kalani, using all their strength, dug in and steered them down the face of the great wave. As they raced through the entrance, the wave spread in all directions and they slowed and found themselves in a confused sea with trees, broken canoes, and Haida bodies.

They continued to paddle hard to get away from the narrows as water began to flow back down the channel. "There will be another wave," Makanunui said. "Head into deeper water."

When the waters had calmed, they brought the squabbling children out from under the mats and rested. Pa'akiki climbed the mast and looked around. "There is another canoe coming," he said.

So the children went back to the shelter, and the crew took up arms and decided to fight rather than run. When the canoe got closer, however, they recognized it as the one they had given to Loa'a and his village.

Loa'a hailed them and they lowered their weapons. "How did you survive?" he asked.

Kolea gestured at Makanunui and said, "We can thank our designer and builder. How is your village?"

"We are in a better place," Loa'a said. "The eastern shore of Haida Gwaii gets little damage from these waves. The earthquake knocked down our totem poles and did some damage to the longhouse, but we were lucky."

"Why did you come out here?" Kolea asked.

"I wanted to see if you survived and if you had, I had decided to go with you." With that, Loa'a grabbed a net bag of his belongings and climbed into the Kio Pa'a. The Haida paddlers bade them farewell and paddled off.

"What now, Kolea?" asked Makanunui.

Kalani broke into the conversation and in a loud voice declaimed, "Now we eat!" And amidst a lot of relieved laughter, they did.

The crew was fatigued after the ordeals of the past week, and Kolea kept the big canoe pointed south with minimal crew at the paddles. The crew napped and gathered their strength for whatever was to come next.

CHAPTER 28

THE BIG WHALING CANOE waited in the calm water miles from shore. Gray whales had been spotted in the area, and the men waited patiently. A fog lay on the water, and in the distance, the men could hear the sound of whales spouting. The eight men in the canoe were experienced whalers. For weeks they had prayed and cleansed their bodies and minds to prepare for this time. The harpoon man stood ready at the bow with a long harpoon tipped with sharpened mussel shells and fitted with barbs fashioned from elk antler. The senior man told them to get ready.

A large male gray whale came out of the fog and blew fifty feet to their right, and without needing further orders, the men brought the canoe up to the speed of the whale and paddled in the direction indicated by their elder. They were off a little when the whale next surfaced, but the elder corrected their course. They paddled steadily and came up on the whale's left side just as he surfaced again. The harpoon man drove his weapon down into the whale just above its left flipper and as the whale rolled, they paid out line from a big basket and paddled backward to get clear of the thrashing whale. At the end of the line were fastened inflated bladders, which they pitched into the water. Then they followed the balloon-like floats, waiting for the whale to tire so they could kill it.

After a time, they lost sight of the floats in the fog but followed the sounds of the wounded whale. They sat still, listening in the calm, when suddenly the whale surfaced next to them and rolled in the water. The protruding harpoon shaft struck the canoe, knocking the harpoon man into the water. In the confusion, the crew lost sight of their companion and paddled to keep clear of the whale. Soon, they could see neither the whale nor the harpoon man.

Nearby, Pa'akiki was on lookout as Kio Pa'a was paddled through the low fog. They were passing a miles-wide entrance to a great body of water and knew from the sounds and the floating kelp that they were near land. He spotted the objects in the water and called Kolea forward.

"Slow and come left," Kolea shouted to the crew.

They found a nearly unconscious man hanging on to some floating globes. They pulled him aboard, and Pualani brought dry cloth and wrapped him together with her body in order to warm him. The floats were moving slowly through the water, and so they followed them.

When the harpoon man came to, he was shocked to see the large people around him and the strange craft. He shouted something, and they all looked puzzled. A shout in the same language came through the fog, and seemingly out of nowhere, a canoe ghosted out of the mist toward them.

The men in the canoe pulled the floats into their canoe and followed the line until they found the exhausted whale. The assistant harpoon man took a sharpened lance and with great care, drove it into a vital area of the great whale and killed it. The whalers used other sharpened lances to seal the whale's mouth so they could tow him and began to paddle away.

The elder in their canoe beckoned the Hawai'ian canoe to follow. Kolea had the Kio Pa'a brought alongside, and the harpoon man was unwrapped and returned to his canoe, but because he was still weak he was unable to paddle. Kepa grabbed a paddle, jumped in, and paddled with the whalers.

The fog began to dissipate as the canoes neared the shore. Kolea could hear the surf and figured the whalers knew the waters, so they followed them into a small coastal bay.

Hundreds of people were waiting on the shore and shouting gleefully at the whale canoe. No one seemed concerned about the double canoe that followed it. Loa'a came to Kolea's shoulder and said, "Ask if you can come ashore." So Kolea spoke in a loud voice and made signs asking to visit the village.

The elder from the whale boat was talking to a man who was dressed in a finely decorated cloak. The man in the cloak pointed to the harpoon man and made signs that were obviously of gratitude. He then waved them ashore, and many people came and helped bring the canoe's bows up onto the beach.

As the voyagers walked into the village, they saw dozens of men and women climbing onto the whale and butchering it. Children ran around the whale, and the atmosphere was that of a huge celebration.

Kolea and his crew were led to a longhouse. Standing before it were huge carved wooden statues of men wearing odd headwear and covered with carved and painted symbols. They were invited in and when they ducked into the round door, they found themselves in a dark, slightly smoky enclosure with sleeping and eating areas all around.

The crew was invited to sit near the fire where large chunks of halibut were pegged onto planks and they were served fish and berries along with the orange-colored eggs of sea urchins. Having been at sea for the past ten days, the Hawai'ians disregarded their gender kapu and dug into the meal with gusto.

Loa'a, who had been a slave of the Salish people, could understand most of the language of the hosts, and he interpreted for Kolea and Makanunui. "This woman appears to speak for the chief. She says that these are Makah people. Their name means something about feeding guests, but I'm not clear about it," he continued. "This is a wealthy tribe that supplies food to other people in trade. They don't appear to fear other tribes, and their totems indicate some history of success in battle."

Kolea nodded and spoke to Makanunui. "I think we can rest here for two days and then move on." Makanunui agreed and they asked the woman if they could stay two days.

She replied, "You saved the life of our best harpoon man. You show no aggressiveness. You are welcome here."

In the evening a great celebration took place. Drummers formed up and dancers enacted dramatic scenes from their mythical and historical events, which the travelers watched and enjoyed. Several dancers were clothed in feathered cloaks and elaborate masks with moving jaws, and they danced near children and tried to frighten them.

As for the Makah, they were fascinated with the size of their visitors and had no compunctions about touching them. At one point, a man asked to purchase Pualani, who seemed to be a favorite among the Makah. The Hawai'ians pointed to Kalani, who was also being groped by villagers. He laughed uproariously and asked what the man would pay. Pualani gave him a whack on his head and everyone enjoyed the show.

As the evening wore on, the Hawai'ians were asked if they had a dance. Makanunui organized the men of the crew, and they retrieved their paddles and performed a dance about voyaging in the southern ocean while Pa'akiki chanted the oli and the Hawai'ian women and children sat and clicked small stones together to create a rhythm. The twirling paddles mesmerized the small children, and when they had finished, there was a cheer as Makah people pounded on the seating platforms. Then the Hawai'ian women danced a hula about the sun rising from the sea.

Early in the morning, the party broke up and the Hawai'ians walked out into a wondrous view. A full moon hung low and shone from a clear sky, and they could see the tall island stacks offshore. They slept in the open on the beach and dreamed of home.

CHAPTER 29

THE THREE WEEKS it took for the Kio Pa'a to wend its way south were eventful. The voyagers met both friendly and unfriendly people along the way as they went ashore to get fresh water and to hunt for food. When conflict appeared, they avoided it. Their urge to get home was beginning to overshadow their urge for adventure. And the experience at Haida Gwaii was in the backs of their minds. Slavery was not unknown in Hawai'i but seeing the way it was practiced in the Pacific Northwest caused them to reconsider its value.

The Kio Pa'a, although well founded and maintained, was making unusual noises while under sail and showing signs of wear. Both Makanunui and Kolea understood that some serious refitting would be necessary before heading west across the ocean. In a brisk wind, they followed the coast until it bore them to the southeast, where the weather warmed considerably. They came upon several large islands that lay in an east-west line before them. They pointed between the biggest of the islands and ran along an eastern shore until they found a bay protected from the swells and wind.

The canoes that came out to meet them were well made and quite maneuverable in the sea, and the occupants were armed. Kolea stood on the forward platform, laid his spear down on the deck, put his hands out in a gesture of friendship, and had his crew do the same. The canoes circled them for a time, and then one drew alongside and a well-muscled man stepped onto Kio Pa'a. He ignored Kolea and walked around the boat, checking everything out. When he saw the children sheltered under their mats, he shouted back to his companions and reached a hand to one of the children. Haunani tensed and prepared to attack the man, but he stroked the child's head and straightened, shouting to his crew, who promptly put down their spears.

Kolea signed to the man that they would like to come ashore and the man understood, stepped back in his canoe, and motioned them to follow. The village of the Chumash, which turned out to be the name of the people, was a busy place. Along the shore, a group was butchering a huge elephant seal, while others were hanging fish fillets on racks to dry. Canoe builders were carving out a redwood log by burning a groove in the top and scraping the charcoal to get to sound wood. The canoe leader gestured for Kolea to follow him, and he was led to a big domed house with a woven exterior. Inside, he was amazed to see that the house structure was made from whalebones.

Among the dozen or so people awaiting him were a woman shaman and a male tribal leader, who signaled Kolea to sit across from him on the reed mats that covered the floor. The first words from the leader were accompanied by welcome signs. The leader pointed at himself and said, "Wot!"

Kolea nodded, repeated the name then replied, "Kolea."

The Wot looked at a sandy area between the mats and drew an outline of a canoe and then some arrows going in all directions and shrugged his shoulders as if asking a question. Kolea indicated he understood and wiped off all of the arrows except the one pointing west. A lively conversation ensued among the Chumash, and the Wot drew his hands apart, asking how far they would travel. As a pure guess, Kolea drew a crescent moon, a half and then a full moon to indicate three weeks. The Wot nodded, welcomed Kolea and spoke to his group, then ordered food to be brought. A bowl of acorn mash and some dried fish and water were brought in and shared by all.

When Kolea had eaten, he walked back to the Kio Pa'a and found Makanunui conversing in sign language with the canoe builders. He was holding a ball of black tar in his hands and watching the caulking being done to a well-used Chumash canoe. Bark fibers soaked with the black tar were being pounded into the joints and seams. Makanunui gave the Chumash boat-builder the jade adze he had been given in the north, and the man showed it to his companions and patted Makanunui on his back, thanking him.

When the word got around, villagers came to meet the Hawai'ians and helped move the Kio Pa'a into an area where it could be pulled ashore for repairs. The children of the travelers had already begun to play with their Chumash counterparts while the adult Hawai'ians rested and began to prepare to re-fit Kio Pa'a for the long voyage home.

On the following day, Makanunui and his new boat-building friend paddled a canoe loaded with crewmembers out to an open beach where they found driftwood logs of all sizes. They chose a seasoned Douglas fir log, rolled it into the water, and towed it back to the village. Makanunui split the log into timbers and they fashioned new wash-strakes for Kio Pa'a. Over the following two weeks, the strakes were drilled and sewn on replacing the worn timbers, and they caulked the seams with live oak fibers and tar. Haunani had been shown an area where reeds grew, and she and her crew harvested dried reeds, carried bundles of them back to the shore, and plaited them into new sails for Kio Pa'a.

The big canoe was launched and final preparations were being made when Makanunui came to Kolea with a worried look on his face. "What's wrong?" Kolea asked.

"I'm in some trouble," Makanunui said. "I've been making love to that woman shaman, and her husband has found out."

Kolea rolled his eyes. Makanunui, without a mate, had been prospecting for lovers all along the coast, and it had finally caught up with him. "Where is the husband?"

Makanunui looked down and shuffled his feet. "He struck his wife and she started dancing a curse on him. He ran into the hills."

"Let me deal with it," Kolea said.

Kolea and Loa'a walked up to the Wot's house and met with the headman outside his door. The Wot called into his house, and the shaman came out. She had a black eye and broken nose and was handed over to Kolea. The Wot flicked all of his fingers, which according to Loa'a was indicating that the shaman was now Kolea's property and that they should leave. With that, Kolea led her back to the boat and handed her over to Makanunui. "She is your responsibility now," he said.

They launched the canoe and paddled out of the bay. Kolea pulled Makanunui aside and asked him why he had chosen the shaman. Makanunui shot him a small smile and said, "You have no idea of the things this woman knows about sex."

"Just keep her out of trouble," Kolea said.

The Kio Pa'a headed south under its new sail. Haunani and Ka'a tended to the shaman's wounds and stuffed some herbal pack into her nostrils to straighten her broken nose as much as they could. She sat and wept as the canoe picked up a good breeze and left the island behind. The three children on the boat came and sat with her, and she calmed down and watched the fur seals swim away as the boat approached a small pod of them.

They passed some larger islands and went farther south as the temperature warmed and the air became moist. After a few days they reached the land's end, turned into the cape on their left, found a sheltered bay, and beached the Kio Pa'a for the night.

That evening, Kolea watched a clear sky as the star Hokule'a passed nearly overhead and set for the travelers a straight line to the west. All of the water containers were filled, and adequate food supplies were stored securely in the boat.

He believed their journey home would begin the following day. The weather gods had other plans.

In the ocean one hundred miles to the south, the temperature of the sea had risen to a critical point, and the humid hot air above the surface began to rise. The spin of the earth formed a counterclockwise spiral, which grew bigger as the morning approached. Within an hour of sunrise, the rising air had gathered enough mass that it formed a circular wind and turned into a hurricane.

* * *

Kolea's first sign of trouble came when two local fishermen came paddling furiously into the bay and began hauling their canoes well up the beach and shouting. The Chumash Shaman pointed at the sky and blew her cheeks out, exhaling a *whoosh*. Kolea recalled the signs of big Hawai'ian tropical storms. He shouted to the crew and they gathered small driftwood logs and placed them in lines on the beach to pull the Kio Pa'a as high above the beach as they could. Then they battened down the gear and waited.

Like most Eastern Pacific hurricanes, this one did not come ashore on the peninsula. But as its eye tracked north along the coast, the winds on the periphery increased and when they hit the tip of the peninsula, sticks and bushes became airborne. The crew ran up the beach to shelter among some large rocks. After a time the winds dropped in intensity and it began to rain. Sheets of rain! Rain they had seldom experienced in such volumes, even in the Hawai'ian islands! It filled the hulls of Kio Pa'a and was running off the stern in gushing twin waterfalls. Those items in the boat that had not been secured spilled onto the beach and were washed into the surging sea. The crew ran to catch them but had to retreat as the surge that accompanied the storm pushed the sea well above its high tide line. So they huddled in their sheltered places and waited.

The rain continued for three hours before the winds finally moved on, rolling out to the west as the storm found cooler water and dissipated. Eventually, the crew came out of their shelters and started bailing the hulls and retrieving what they could. A shout came from the rocky area, and Kolea ran up the beach to find Haunani and Pa'akiki holding Ka'a's limp body. Her leg was swollen and badly discolored. Pa'akiki was weeping and gnashing his teeth.

The Chumash shaman took one look at Ka'a's wound and drew back. She found a stick with a small crook on its end and began to fish around in the rock with it. Within a minute or so she drew an angry rattlesnake out, dropped it on a stone and pinned it behind its head with the stick while she severed its head with a small knife. The Hawai'ians had never seen such a creature and drew back as she picked up the snake's head and carefully opened its jaws. She pointed at the twin fangs, tossed the head to the still-writhing body, and pointed to the telltale fang marks in Ka'a's leg.

Everyone left the rocky area and placed the three children on the Kio Pa'a's platform for safety. Drawing a poultice from her bag, the shaman placed it onto Ka'a's swelling wound. Then she brought forth a stone tube, placed it on the fang marks, and sucked on one end to draw some of the fluid out, spitting to make sure none remained in her mouth. She had Ka'a laid out in a cool area and sat with her, changing the poultice periodically until the swelling stopped.

The two native fishermen had observed the events and launched their canoes. Kolea and Makanunui took stock of the damage and began an inventory of the cargo. The dried fish supplies were soaked, but the calm air following the storm had lost its moisture so they hung the fish on bushes and flat stones to dry again.

The big loss was their paddles. Many had washed into the sea, and Makanunui was banging his palm against his head, wondering where he would find adequate wood to carve new ones.

As they continued their cleanup, their luck changed. The two fishermen returned, paddling into the bay with their canoes loaded with the travelers' paddles and lauhala mats they had salvaged from the beaches within a few miles of the bay. The Chumash shaman through Haunani interpreted, "They say they are sorry about your woman. They stay here alone for long periods of time and were happy to see people. I believe they are lonely." To thank the fishermen, Kepa brought them some of the fishing lures he had fashioned and invited them to join them in a meal.

On the third day in the bay, the fish and supplies had dried sufficiently, and the twin-hulled canoe had been packed and relaunched. The calm that followed the hurricane had morphed into a fair wind blowing along the coast, and the Kio Pa'a's crew finally sailed away from the continent they had been living on for seven years.

CHAPTER 30

THE WIND BLEW STEADY from the northwest. The great canoe, carrying its two crab-claw sails, was not capable of tacking into the wind, and so they sailed southwest and waited for the winds to change.

Ka'a had survived the snake bite but had developed a permanent limp from the deadening of some of the flesh in her leg. When Pa'akiki was not taking his duty turns, he spent his time with his daughter La'a kea, teaching her chants and painting verbal pictures of the child's home-to-be. By the seventh day at sea, Kepa could not catch fish in the open sea, but they captured a sea turtle and cooked it in their fire pit.

Birds had disappeared. Perhaps once each day, a brown booby would fly by them, but the sea seemed barren of any lives but their own.

Makanunui and the Chumash shaman stayed apart. She had made friends with the women of the crew, was learning the language of the Hawai'ians, and she took part in the daily work of repairing and maintaining the Kio Pa'a.

On their eighth day at sea, the winds shifted, and they caught the trade winds and picked up speed. As they surfed the big waves and climbed up the back sides, Kalani required additional steersmen, and Kolea, Pualani, and others took watches on the big steering paddle to give Kalani some rest. During the days, they would simply go with the direction of the trade winds, and on clear or partially clear nights they would correct to Hokolea's path through the night sky and keep an eye on the Kio Pa'a's namesake, the polar star. Rain squalls came often enough to keep them supplied with water, but after three weeks at sea, the rations were nearly gone and were being saved for the children.

The fatigued and hungry crew was occupied with watching the confusing wave patterns when little La'a kea spotted the bird. The child was lying on her back when she saw high above them a bird she had never seen before. The bird floated on the wind and appeared to stay in the same spot without moving its wings. "Look, Father," she said.

"What is it," Pa'akiki answered from his paddle station.

"Look up," she said.

Pa'akiki did and saw that it was a great frigate bird, a sight that filled him with glee. "Iwa! Iwa!" he shouted. Makanunui climbed into a hull and lay on the bottom, feeling the wave patterns for five minutes. When he came up he pointed in a westerly direction and said, "Land is that way." Kalani corrected course, and the crew climbed up onto the deck-platform and scanned the horizon.

As they watched, other birds began to appear, and Kolea watched them and had the canoe steered in the direction of those carrying small fish in their bills. At the first sight of land, they lowered the sail to make themselves less visible and paddled toward it. The first recognizable landmark was the long ridge of the Koolau Mountains, and they knew they had navigated their way back to Oahu.

Makanunui asked Kalani, "Can you steer us through the reefs in the darkness?"

"If there are fires to guide me, I can," he replied.

They waited until dusk and let the trade winds and their muffled paddles carry them into Kaneohe Bay. To ensure their safety, Kolea prepared everyone for any possible combat, secured the children in the shelter and kept the Kio Pa'a near the bay entrance for the night.

In the morning, canoes from the village came out. In the bow of one canoe was a young chief. Makanunui recognized him as the man who had hurled the spear across the assemblage during their last trip, seven years previous. Makanunui shouted a request to visit, and the young chief waved them ashore.

The crew paddled Kio Pa'a to the beach and were met by villagers who watched the strangest collection of people they had ever seen stagger onto the beach on sea legs. The Tlingit and Chumash women were greeted with great curiosity and welcoming gestures. Children gathered around and asked many questions.

At long last home, many of the crew kneeled on the beach and uttered words of thanks. The people of the village brought flowers, food, and shell leis and embraced the travelers, welcoming them back.

Kolea sought out the young chief and asked him about Chief Kanaka wai wai. "He died last year while he was fishing," the young chief said. "It was a good death, and we took his remains to a secret place. I am now the chief of the village." The new chief's name was Naukana. He invited Kolea and Makanunui to eat with him and saw that their crew was fed and cared for.

When they had eaten, Naukana looked down and then spoke in a soft voice. "I have been expecting you," he said. "Your two mothers, the Owl Woman, Pueo, and another were brought here some months ago. Pueo gave me a message for you and made me swear not to give it to anyone else. She simply said to tell you, 'Pelekunu. Come alone.' "

Kolea digested the information and looked at Naukana. "And what do you know of my father Ko'i?"

Naukana said, "The blind warrior was killed in a battle at Halawa. He covered a retreat while your mother escaped. Mahi has long raided villages on Molokai, looking for you, but now he has gone back to Maui."

"Any news of my father?" Makanunui asked.

"Your father is like the wisest of the mountain pigs," he said. "His warriors are in the mountains on Molokai and every time Mahi thinks he has him cornered, the old man slips away."

Makanunui looked at Kolea, and what he saw gave him pause. The calmness that had sustained them during their voyage was replaced with a burning look that required no explanation. Kolea thanked Naukana, rose and walked out onto the beach, where he began to run and soon disappeared. Makanunui returned to the canoe and shared the bad news with his crew.

In two hours, an exhausted Kolea returned. "Can you get us a small canoe?" he asked.

CHAPTER 31

DURING THE FOLLOWING WEEK, they hauled the Kio Pa'a onto the beach for maintenance, and Makanunui cleaned and repaired a worn-out smaller canoe he had been given. The canoe carried twelve paddlers, so the Molokai people prepared to go home and find their families. Each day, Kolea led them on a run, and they lifted stones and practiced with the short spears as Ko'i had taught them. At the end of the second week they were ready, and they passed their children to Oahu crewmembers and left. The canoe bucked into the oncoming waves, but the crew had recovered their strength, and the long days of paddling in the ocean caused them to work together with ease.

After they had crossed the channel between islands they hugged the shore and stopped for the night on the beach near Kalaupapa. Before the sun was up, they had rounded the peninsula and were headed for Halawa. About halfway there, Kolea nodded at Makanunui, kissed Haunani good-bye, grabbed his short spear, and dropped over the side of the canoe. As they paddled on, they saw him swimming to the notch that opened into Pelekunu Valley.

The old woman and her younger companion watched from their hiding spot as the canoe sped away. There wasn't much of a beach, and they saw Kolea wait for a surge of water to lift him and haul himself onto the rocky shelf at the water's edge. "He is a handsome and powerful man like his father," the younger woman said.

"Yes, he is," said Pueo. "And his other father taught him well, or he would not have returned to us."

Kolea could feel her presence, and he walked up the stream as the two women emerged from their hiding place. He hugged Pueo gently. The hard muscles that had made her such a powerful woman were gone. But still she carried the power centered in her gut and she wept as he held her.

"This is your mother, Aala," Pueo said. "She wept when I took her from you and she wept when you came out of the sea." Kolea embraced her and breathed an aloha, mingling his breath with hers.

"I am too old to care about the kapu," Pueo said. "Come and eat with us and tell me of your voyage."

"I will," Kolea replied. "But after we eat you must first tell me how Ko'i died."

Pueo saw and felt the power of Kolea's force, his mana, and she felt a keen sensation of good. They sat and ate, and when they had finished she told the story of Ko'i's last day.

"Mahi's warriors came from the sea. Iaea was prepared, but another force sneaked down the trail and attacked his rear. Iaea and much of his village escaped into the valleys and went to hiding places he had established in the event of an attack."

"And Ko'i?" Kolea asked.

"Ko'i sent me away and told me he would not fare well on the run and he would make Mahi's warriors pay," Pueo continued. "He hid in the house, and from what I was told, he killed five of those who were searching the village. It is said that when the leader of the raid came to finish him off after Ko'i had been wounded, Ko'i laughed and dislocated the man's arm so badly that his arm is even now worthless to him. They killed him while he laughed in their faces."

Kolea nodded and said, "Ko'i once told me that he would prefer to die in battle than to end up a feeble blind man."

He paused. "Iaea was responsible for getting rid of Mahi's enemies," he said. "But Mahi's rage over not killing me has made him crazier than he already was. He hunts his allies as well as me. When I am ready, he will get the opportunity to find me."

And with that, the two women sat with him for most of the night and listened to the tales of Kolea's travels to the north, the adventures on the way south, and the strange people he had encountered.

When Kolea mentioned that he had a son to bring to them, both women teared up.

In the morning, Pueo told Kolea how to find Iaea and his villagers. She told him that her abilities to help him were greatly reduced as she had aged, but she retained an ability to give him warnings when she was called upon. Kolea nodded and said, "I am home, Pueo. And I am filled with the mana given to me by my mother and father, and the power and training given by you and Ko'i. I am ready." He embraced them both and walked up the narrow valley into the forest.

*   *   *

Kolea followed the wild pig trails up and down the ridges without tiring. His body seemed infused with a renewed spirit. His first task was to find Makanunui and the others. He walked inside the forest and worked his way down to the now-abandoned village at Halawa.

Some sixth sense told him something was wrong as he approached the village. He smelled the warriors before he could see them. They were watching the beach where Makanunui and the others had spent the night. Kolea skirted the watchers, and when he was some distance away, he made a bird sound of alarm. Makanunui picked up the sound and as casually as he could he warned the others to continue what they were doing but to have their weapons nearby.

Kolea scouted the warriors and counted fifteen. He waited until one of the watchers walked back to relieve himself. The man did not see him as the garrote snaked around his neck. He was dead in a few seconds and was dragged into the bushes. When his companion came to find him, he suffered the same fate, and when the leader realized two of his men were gone, he went back to find them.

By then, Kolea had gone to the other end of the watcher's line and decided the odds were good enough. He shouted and attacked the end of the line and saw Makanunui and the others running toward him.

Kolea dropped down and swung the butt of his spear into his opponent's knee, disabling him. The second, more experienced warrior came at Kolea with an axe and kept himself out of range, sparring with him. Kolea backed up as if in retreat, faked a fall, and when the warrior advanced, he rose up with a stone and threw it into the warrior's face. When the man raised his hands to protect his face, Kolea drove his spear into his chest and took the axe from the other man's hands.

Kalani, Makanunui, and the others joined the fray and killed two more warriors. Three others escaped but the rest had surrendered. The leader, seeing what had happened, ran up the trail to escape. Makanunui started after him but Kolea stopped him. "Let him go. He will bring Mahi and we will fight him on the ground of our choosing rather than his."

Kolea gathered the surviving warriors and spoke to them. "Mahi sends you after me and tells you that I murdered his father. But Mahi killed his father and blamed me. He has lied to you. Look into my eyes and you will know I speak the truth." He walked up and down the captives' line and said, "You may join us, or we will send you back to Maui, where you can follow your brave leader who has run away and left you. If you go, our next meeting will be your last."

The eldest of the warriors looked at Kolea and said, "I believe this man." And the rest agreed and said they would join him. Kolea chanted a blessing over the dead, and they buried them under stones outside the village.

They hauled their canoe into the forest and walked up the stream bed into the mountains. After crossing two steep ridges, they came to the valley Pueo had described. "Your father will have sentries and warriors waiting. Go by yourself and when he knows it is you, call us down," Kolea said to Makanunui.

Makanunui started down a pig trail and was soon challenged by a sentry. "I am Makanunui, son of Iaea," he said in a loud voice.

Warriors who had been hidden in the thick forest came out and looked him over. Two of them recognized him. "We thought you were dead," they said.

"Someday, but not yet," he replied. "I have companions." He whistled and the rest joined him.

They were led to a hidden village in a small valley. Iaea had heard the commotion and met his son with a strong embrace. The chief had aged, but his resolve was still there. "I had no doubt of your return," he told Makanunui.

"What of my mother?"

"She is dead," Iaea said. "Killed while we escaped from Mahi's trap."

Tears came to Makanunui's eyes and he looked at his father. "There will come a time when Mahi will pay for his crimes."

Iaea embraced Kolea and gathered the crew at his temporary village and they ate together. Haunani had found her mother, and after eating, they joined the men and listened as Pa'akiki told stories of their fantastic journey.

The next morning Iaea awoke to the sounds of people exercising. He walked from his shelter and saw Kolea, Makanunui, and the others from their crew lifting stones and stretching their muscles. Haunani and Pualani were off to one side, sparring with short spears.

Iaea watched the exercises and waited until they were finished. He motioned Kolea to him and they sat on a flat rock and talked. "I have a plan to get my island back and to take out Mahi and his army," Iaea said. "But I have no war chief capable of carrying it out." Kolea nodded. "I want you to train my warriors and lead them in battle."

Kolea gathered his thoughts and said, "I can train them, and I can lead them in battle. But you should not underestimate your son. Makanunui has inherited your strategic abilities."

Iaea nodded. "That is what I surmised. I will work out a plan with him."

Kolea agreed and said, "Makanunui is also the cleverest fighter I know. He was often underestimated by enemy fighters, and those who did so are dead. I also want Pualani and Haunani to train women warriors. We will probably have to fight greater numbers and will need the women at times."

Iaea agreed, and the two men joined the others, where Iaea gave orders to his people to prepare for the coming battle.

CHAPTER 32

IN THE FOLLOWING MONTHS, Kolea drove and trained Iaea's warriors until they were as fit as his own crew. Each morning, they ran up and down the steep slopes of their hidden valley and spent time lifting stones and practicing with the long and short spears. In the afternoon, they grappled and learned the lua fighting techniques. At the same time the women were learning spear fighting and some of Pualani's lethal fighting techniques. Makanunui taught them Ko'i's paddle fighting techniques, and they carved new paddles to his patterns.

During one of the practice sessions, Kolea overheard a young warrior bragging that the women could not really fight as well as even he, a novice, could. Kolea called him out and beckoned Pualani over to his training ground.

Kolea related what had been said and Pualani looked over the cocky warrior. "Here is a wager," she said. "Short spears. If I win, you strip naked and crawl across this ground."

"What if I win?" asked the youngster. Before the words were out of his mouth, Pualani had made a quick move with her spear, whipped his spear from his grip, spun him around, and slammed him to the ground on his belly.

She leaned in and said into his ear, "If you win I will turn into a giant pig with wings and fly to Oahu." Then she helped the boy up.

When another young warrior laughed, Pualani walked to him and stared into his face for a few seconds. The young man looked down at the ground, and she eyed all the others before she walked back to the women. Thereafter, there was no more of such talk from the young men.

The next day, Iaea's spies told him that Mahi's warriors had spotted the village. Within four hours the entire village was gone, as if they had never existed. Iaea cautioned Kolea not to begin a battle until he was fully prepared, and so Makanunui and Kolea found a hiding post and watched the empty village.

On the second day, Mahi's men came. More than two hundred warriors in two groups crossed into the valley and were disappointed to find it empty. They searched the area but could find no trail to follow. After holding a conference, they went back in the direction from whence they had come.

Makanunui started to leave, but Kolea signaled for him to stay hidden. An owl had flown low over them and then flown in ever-smaller circles over a spot in the forest where the warriors had met. "Wait here. If you see anyone move, give me a bird call," Kolea said.

Makanunui nodded and Kolea disappeared into the bushes. In half an hour, he returned with a man who had stayed behind as an observer. The man's arms were trussed up, and he was gagged with a piece of cloth. Kolea led him by a cord looped around the man's neck. The three climbed to the ridge and waited an hour to make certain they were not followed and then walked to the new site of their mobile village.

When they reached the new encampment, Kolea interrogated the warrior. He threatened the man with grievous harm and the man clamped up. "Bring him to my father," Makanunui said.

Iaea had the bindings taken off the man and had food brought to him. He sat with the man and asked him about his family. When the man began to relax after he had eaten, he spoke to Iaea. The captive said he was from Waiehu on Maui, with a group of men sent to find Pueo and Kolea and that Mahi, the king, was preparing a fleet with which to invade Molokai and then Oahu. Iaea told the man he would spare his life and ordered him released.

Kolea came to Iaea and asked why he had let the man go. "He will give away our location," he said.

"Perhaps he will," Iaea replied. "And Mahi will come with an army so large, we will be unable to defeat him in a pitched battle. But we will not be here when he comes. Bring Makanunui and let us figure a way through this."

During the following week, Iaea sent runners to the other chiefs who had been moving just ahead of the Maui warriors and hiding in some of the inaccessible windward valleys of Molokai. Makanunui was sent to retrieve the Kio Pa'a and to inform the Oahu chiefs of Mahi's intent. Then he instructed Kolea. And their plan was put into action.

CHAPTER 33

OBSERVERS SAW THE FLEET of war canoes coming across the channel from Maui and sent runners to inform Kolea and Iaea. Four big war canoes and a fleet of smaller outriggers were headed for Halawa. Mahi landed his troops on the beach at Halawa and sent out small scouting patrols to locate the moving villages. One of them was sent to the location described by the warrior Iaea had released.

The patrol was working their way up a ridge when they heard the sounds of women talking and laughing. The sound was coming from the steep windward cliffs to the left of their path. Gesturing for silence, the leader followed the sounds into a narrow stream course that led to the base of the cliff. The men stood there puzzled and discovered that they had been following an echo of sounds coming from the other side of the valley.

Suddenly, a deep voice came from a wind-carved cave above them, and when the men looked up a horrible figure, chanting in a deep voice, emerged. The figure was the size of a short man but appeared to be feathered and had the face of a strange bird whose beak began clapping loudly. Loud buzzing sounds followed from the top of the cliff, and terrified, the warriors began to run. As they entered the narrows, the women on the cliffs far above heaved rocks down upon them, striking damaging blows and killing two of the men.

In the cave, Pa'akiki removed the Lekwiltok shaman's helmet-mask and winged cloak, stowed them back in their box, and led the two young warriors with him down to the narrows, where they finished off the wounded warriors and dragged their bodies into the brush. The men who escaped returned to the main army with their story.

Mahi was enraged. He struck the patrol leader with his axe and killed him instantly. Facing his troops, he screamed, "There is no magic here. Only trickery! We will find the killer of my father, and we will make him and his people plead for death." He instructed a contingent to guard the canoes and led his army up the main valley behind Halawa.

The afternoon brought a warm breeze to the bay in front of Halawa, and the canoe guards whiled away their time at a big konane stone. Two men sat and manipulated the white and black game pieces, wagering on the outcome of the games being played. The canoes were in a line along the inner beach with their sterns afloat in the sheltered waters.

From the forest, Haunani and two younger women emerged, dropped their garments, and walked into the fresh water some distance from the canoe guards. The guard's attention was distracted, and two of the men started toward the women. "Wait," the leader said. "It might be a trap. Two of you go and bring them back and we'll question them and have some fun as well."

The two warriors walked to the stream and followed it to where the three women were bathing. "Get out of there and come with us," one of the men said. The three smiling women agreed and walked naked from the water and down to the canoes.

The guard's leader scanned the forest and surroundings looking for some kind of trap, but his eyes and those of all of his men kept going back to the lovely women. If he had eyes in the back of his head, he would have seen Makanunui and his crew swimming silently across the bay and creeping up through the fleet of canoes. One of the guards saw them, but it was too late. Makanunui brought down the leader with his spear. The others scrambled to give battle but were soon subdued.

Makanunui whistled, and a large crowd of women and young people came out of the forest and helped push the four war canoes into the bay. Makanunui assigned crewmembers as captains, and the women and young people paddled the big canoes out of the bay where Kio Pa'a was waiting. Crewmembers were distributed among the canoes, and they set the sails and caught the trade winds.

In the afternoon, the canoes stopped at the entrance to Pelekunu Valley and many villagers and warriors swam from the beach and loaded the canoes to capacity. The whole fleet then sailed off, rounded the peninsula at Kalaupapa, and the people swam ashore and were greeted by Iaea, Kolea, and three other chiefs. Much of the population of Molokai was now on this big peninsula. They had either come in the big canoes, paddled their outrigger canoes from the leeward side of the island or had scrambled and slid down the difficult trail from the cliffs high above.

There was no strategic advantage to be had by anyone invading Kalaupapa, as the peninsula was a natural fortress. There was a beach of sorts at the east end at Kalawao where an attack could be made, but the landing was difficult in the rocky surf. The tall cliffs protected the rest of the peninsula so a land-based invasion would require a single file scramble down a very steep trail, making the invaders vulnerable to being picked off one at a time.

The chiefs sat in conference. Iaea spoke first. "Mahi will soon discover where we are. If he goes home, he will bring back a bigger army and we will suffer a disadvantage in a traditional fight."

"Let us get after him on our own ground," one of the other chiefs said. "We are tired of running from place to place."

Iaea looked at Kolea. "What do you think, Kolea?"

"Pueo tells me that Mahi has already discovered our whereabouts," Kolea replied. "I want to know Makanunui's opinion."

Makanunui stood up and grabbed a sharp stick. He drew a map of Molokai. "Mahi will not attack us here. He will go back to Maui, and when he returns it will not be possible to use clever moves to beat him. Although we have an advantage in a battle on our ground, sheer numbers will overtake us."

He paused and looked at Kolea. "Our place of advantage is actually the sea. Our crew has experienced every kind of sea possible, including two sea battles in the north. And we could sail circles around Mahi's canoes."

Kolea nodded. "I would attack him at sea. We don't have the time to train additional crews to attack him now," he said. "I would let him ferry as many of his warriors back to Maui as he can. When he has left, I would gather in those he cannot fit in the outriggers. I would like the chance to turn them to our side. We can have our canoes trained by the time Mahi gets his next invasion prepared." The chiefs discussed the plan and agreed that it made sense.

When Mahi loaded his army on the few remaining outriggers, he took his best warriors and left the rest. Though he told them he would return for them, it was widely believed that they would be abandoned. Many of the warriors served Mahi out of fear rather than loyalty, and when the Molokai warriors came into the valley, they lined up in a defensive formation and expected the worst. The sides lined up across from one another, and the traditional insults were shouted back and forth as each side gathered their courage to attack.

The Maui warriors watched as a powerful-looking chief walked out from the other side. He was scarred and tattooed and carried a war axe and a short spear. The man spoke, and his voice was clear. "I am Kolea, son of King Nanoa and Aalaonaona of Molokai." He then recited his genealogy as he had learned it from Pueo. When he was finished he said, "I have come back from a long voyage in order to right a wrong. Many years ago, in a blood-lust rage, my half-brother tried to kill me but killed our father instead. He falsely blamed me and has hunted me for years. His hunt is over. I will kill him this year. If you join me, you will no longer be under the command of a despot."

Many of the Maui warriors had heard similar stories from women with whom Pueo had spoken. Others were simply tired of the cruelty of their king. Most put down their weapons and came across the ground. From the remainder came a growl, and a powerful-looking man with many scars strode into the clearing. He shouted his genealogies and challenged Kolea.

Weapons were handed to nearby warriors and the two circled one another before they came at each other in a rush. The Maui fighter struck first, breaking Kolea's nose with a head-butt. Kolea backed away and wiped the blood from his nose. The pain was intense, but as Ko'i had taught him, he put it in a mental compartment and grappled with the man.

Kolea's opponent was an experienced lua fighter. He had been left behind because he was a constant troublemaker. He grabbed

Kolea around the torso in a powerful hold, but as he lifted him, Kolea smashed an elbow into his eye socket, and the man let go and grabbed for his face.

It was his last mistake. Kolea whipped the man's arm in a painful direction and dislocated his shoulder. Then he grabbed him around the torso, lifted him, and smashed him to the ground. He reached an arm around the man's neck and choked him until he was dead. When Kolea stood, the remainder of the Maui warriors came over and joined the rest.

CHAPTER 34

LOOKOUTS HAD BEEN posted high on the eastern side of Molokai and charged with watching. Iaea also sent spies to Maui to watch Mahi's preparations. Makanunui worked on the war canoes. He fastened hardwood prows that projected at an angle above the water, and he inlaid sharpened basalt pieces in the bow structures. Pa'akiki and Kalani were given charge of two of the boats, and they trained their crews with daily sailings.

Kepa, the former assassin, had become the best sailor of all and was given command of the third canoe. Makanunui captained the Kio Pa'a, and Kolea was in charge of the fighters on all of the boats. The tale of his battle with the Maui lua fighter had spread among the troops, and now he was respected by the older fighters as well as the young ones. Haunani told Kolea that he now looked more like a warrior with two blackened eyes and a bent nose, which she had stuffed with healing herbs to straighten.

Each morning to become stronger, the warriors ran and climbed the slopes before lifting stones, mock fighting, and spear work. Pualani was in charge of a troop of women and young men who would guard the villages in the absence of the boats, and she trained them as well. A contingent of fighters who were not good at sea were sent to camp at the top of the cliffs to guard against surprise from the landside.

By the end of the first month, the crews were becoming competent with the big canoes. They could sail in the rough winds and paddle to maneuver in battle. The sails could be spilled of wind in a short time and furled to the mast as the paddlers took over. They trained with the fighting paddles Makanunui had designed.

Fifty days after the Maui soldiers had left, reports started to filter in that Mahi was ready for war. He had acquired all of the war canoes from chiefs of all the Maui villages and was supplying a corps twice the size of Molokai's. Kolea inspected his warriors, found them ready, and outlined the battle plan he and Makanunui had developed. And then they did what warriors have done everywhere; they waited.

Day after day they waited, with no news. And then it happened. A runner came to the top of the cliff and blew a message in his conch shell and the navy launched their canoes. The launch took place in the predawn darkness as they paddled directly north and away from the island. They navigated by stars and moved well upwind from the island until they could see only the tops of the cliffs. The sails were furled but made ready.

Mahi's fleet of canoes was crossing the channel between Maui and Molokai, expecting the canoes to come either from Halawa or the Kalaupapa area, He sought the advantage of being under sail upwind from the defenders, but he saw no canoes coming out and assumed he was in a position to surprise them. When the fleet was off Halawa, a fire showed up on top of the cliffs and Mahi assumed the warning was up and they would have no element of surprise. Still he was not worried.

The surprise came from the open sea. When the signal fire was lit, Makanunui ordered the sails unfurled, and the paddlers drove the boat forward in front of the strong and steady trade winds. They charged into Mahi's fleet from upwind. Makanunui steered Kio Pa'a right at the stern of the last canoe and the new bow-piece sheared off the stern of the closest hull and pitched the steersman into the water with his paddle. The great canoe was disabled and its crew, occupied with saving the boat, was attacked by the Molokai warriors and subdued quickly. Kepa's canoe had made a similar attack and disabled another canoe and was in a broad side battle with a third. The plight of the two disabled canoes evened the odds.

The two other Molokai canoes had missed their marks and their crews were fighting hand to hand. Kalani's crew included Loa'a, who stood in the bow of the canoe using a Haida canoe smashing stone. The heavy ring he had fashioned from coarse lava stone was swung on the end of a stout rope and it smashed through a thin part of his opponent's canoe, causing its occupants to bail water. Kalani's disciplined fighters boarded with short spears and paddles and drove some of the Maui warriors into the sea. Others surrendered.

Kolea scanned the battle and spotted the canoe he was looking for. It had the Maui war god's image high on the bow of one hull. He pointed at it and Makanunui had the Kio Pa'a paddled to it. The two canoes stood off from one another as Mahi, surrounded by his spearmen and lua fighters, shouted his genealogy and abuses at Kolea. In a calm deep voice, Kolea recited his family as well and said, "The false king is a liar and a coward. He killed our father and blamed me."

As the canoes drifted closer together, spears appeared all along the gunwale of the Maui canoe. There was no response from Kio Pa'a's paddlers, and the Maui warriors began yelling at them and laughing. Just as the canoes closed Makanunui yelled a command and his warriors on the platform hurled fist-sized stones at the Maui paddlers who raised their spears in disarray.

The Kio Pa'a paddlers, in response to a second command, did a draw stroke, pulling themselves under the long spears, pulled their paddles from the water and in unison began slicing into the Maui paddlers with the sharp edges of their paddles. On a third command they reversed the paddles and stabbed into their opponents with the sharpened upper end. Kolea shouted and led his warriors from the platform, boarded the other canoe, and engaged the spearmen surrounding Mahi. One lua fighter guarding the king grabbed Kolea but immediately let go when one of Makanunui's spears caught him in his rib cage.

As the battle raged back and forth on the two boats, Kolea, armed with two of Ko'i's war axes, smashed his way onto Mahi's platform and dispatched the last lua fighter with two blows from his axes.

Now the half-brothers faced each other. Mahi, armed with a short spear and a pahoa dagger, faced Kolea. "No weapons," he said, laying down his spear and knife.

Kolea dropped the axes and stood ready. "Stop!" they both yelled to their men, and the fighting ceased as everyone eyed the two big men circling each other.

Mahi feinted a move and tried to grapple, but Kolea slipped out of it and continued to move around, looking for weaknesses that would give him an advantage over the bigger and more experienced Mahi. He found that Mahi's upper body was well balanced, but he favored a position with one foot always forward. Kolea switched direction to circle around the outer side of Mahi's lead and charged him.

But Mahi had been faking. He drew back the lead foot and delivered a blow to the side of Kolea's head, knocking him to the deck. And then he was on top of Kolea, trying to find a grip.

Kolea was stunned but set the pain aside, grabbed Mahi's foot, and dislocated his big toe. Mahi screamed and Kolea escaped from his grip. Mahi jumped up favoring his uninjured foot, and Kolea rose from the deck with a sidekick that landed on the ankle of Mahi's planted foot.

As the Maui king was falling, he grabbed a cord hidden in his belt and wrapped it around Kolea's neck, taking him to the deck. Kolea could feel himself losing consciousness, but he recalled Ko'i's admonition, "A real fighter will never give up!"

He reached behind, grasped Mahi's testicles, and yanked hard. When Mahi screamed and let go, Kolea got a finger under the cord and ripped it loose. He stood up, got a hold on Mahi's head, and with all of the strength from all of the stones he had lifted over the years, and all of the anger over Ko'i's death, he rammed Mahi's head into the mast over and over until he no longer moved.

Kolea picked Mahi's body up and walked to the bow of the canoe, holding him up for all to see. Then he tied an anchor stone to Mahi's neck and kicked his body into the sea. He removed the Maui war god image from its niche above the bow and held it up for all to see. And then he wrapped it in its cloth cover, and in so doing, he declared the fight over.

The warriors in the other canoes ceased fighting, and Kolea shouted orders that all combatants should be pulled from the water and the killing should end. When he turned, he found that all of the fighters had prostrated themselves and that he was now the king of Maui.

Kolea also recognized that they had drifted nearly onto the beach at Kalawao and ordered the undamaged canoes to paddle around the peninsula, land and care for the wounded of both sides. Then he dispatched Pa'akiki's canoe to go back along the coast and pick up those who had either swum ashore or drifted in on the wreckage.

The news had reached Kalaupapa by the time Kolea arrived, and people gave way and many prostrated themselves before him at the landing. Kolea found Haunani in a grass shelter weeping next to the wrapped body of a small person. "Pueo?" he asked, sorrow in his heart.

Haunani nodded. "She had me help her to the top of the little volcano in the middle of Kalaupapa, and she watched the battle. She was chanting quietly throughout the battle and when it appeared to be over, she smiled and slumped forward dead."

All of the emotions of the day came up from Kolea's gut and he sat next to Pueo's body and wept.

Kaupo, Ten years later

The sails of the big double-hulled canoe had been spotted coming from the south and Kolea had canoes launched and prepared for whatever was coming, but he had a feeling that it was Makanunui. The big heiau he had ordered constructed ten years before was close to his house and so he climbed it and watched the canoe come closer. The men and women on the voyaging canoe were shouting greetings to those meeting them in the outriggers, and a welcoming crowd began to gather on the beach. Kolea climbed back down to the house, donned a ceremonial feather cloak, and made his way to the landing.

On the bow of one hull stood Makanunui, dressed in some strange costume and flanked by two beautiful Tahitian women. Haunani had joined Kolea along with Nene, who was now a strapping seventeen-year-old. Haunani was laughing at the scene before them, and Kolea could not help himself from doing the same. Makanunui stepped ashore and knelt before Kolea, who grabbed him by the shoulders and embraced him. The Tahitian women prostrated themselves.

Makanunui whispered to Kolea, "They are doing that for me, not you. Don't tell them. They think I am more important than you." And then the two friends joined the others for a celebration and some serious story telling.

Pau

GLOSSARY

Here is a glossary of some Hawai'ian words used in *Kolea,* as adapted from Pukui and Elbert, *Hawaiian Dictionary* (1986, University of Hawaii Press)

ala'ea: Red soil with iron mixed with salt.
ali'i: Regal. Refers to chiefs and other leaders.
ama: Outrigger float
amakihi: Small honeycreeper, a native bird
anu'enue: Rainbow, known as also the Brocken Spectre
auwe: An interjection of surprise
hala: Pandanus tree
halau wa'a: Canoe shed
hanai: Adoption, often unofficial foster parenting
heiau: Stone platform for worship
iako: Arm connecting outrigger to canoe or second canoe
ihe: A spear
i'iwi: Red honeycreeper, a native bird
imu: Underground oven
kahinali'i: Tsunami
iwa: Frigate bird
kahuna kalai wa'a: Priest, or canoe builder
kapa: Tapa cloth pounded from bark
kapu: Prohibition
kauila: A hardwood used in weapons and tools

Kio pa'a: Polaris, the North Star
ko'i: Axe or adze
ko'i kupa: Finishing adze
koa: Warrior
kohola: Humpbacked whale
komo mai e ai: "Welcome, come and eat"
konane: Checkers-like game played on a flat stone or board
kukae ilio: Dog excrement
kukui: Candlenut tree with many uses
kuli kuli o'e: Shut up!
kumu: Teacher
kupuna: Grandparent or ancestor
lauhala: Pandanus leaf used in plaited matting and sails
lawe olelo: Gossip
lua: In this context, a vicious style of fighting; a martial art
malolo: Flying fish
mamane: A leguminous bush or tree found high on the mountains
mana: Power, authority often considered inherited
manini: Black and white striped fishes
mo'o: Lizard or reptile
mele: Song or chant
nene: Hawai'ian goose
oha wai nui: Medicinal plant
o'o: Yellow-tufted black bird
ohia lehua: A flowering tree
olona: Shrub with bark used in making cordage
opelu: A fish, mackerel scad
paele: Black, to darken
pahoa: A short dagger
palaoa: A white ivory whale tooth pendant
pa'u: Skirt
pau: Finished
pueo: Short-eared owl
pupule: Crazy
taro: A staple food crop
ti: A plant with leaves of many uses
wa'a: Canoe
wauke: Paper mulberry bush, bark pounded into kapa

MORE GREAT READS
FROM BOOKTROPE

Paradigm Shift **by Bill Ellis** (Historical Fiction) A rich blend of social history, drama, love, passion and determination, Ellis delivers a powerful page-turner about the struggles and perseverance to overcome all odds.

Revontuli **by Andrew Eddy** (Historical Fiction) Inspired by true events, Revontuli depicts one of the last untold stories of World War II: the burning of the Finnmark. Marit, a strong-willed Sami, comes of age and shares a forbidden romance with the German soldier occupying her home.

Sweet Song **by Terry Persun** (Historical Fiction) This tale of a mixed-race man passing as white in post-Civil-War America speaks from the heart about where we've come from and who we are.

The Secrets of Casanova **by Greg Michaels** (Historical Fiction) Loosely inspired by Casanova's life, this novel thrusts the reader into an adventure overflowing with intrigue, peril, and passion.

Discover more books and learn about our
new approach to publishing at **www.booktrope.com**.

CPSIA information can be obtained
at www.ICGtesting.com
Printed in the USA
FSOW01n1253280815
10493FS